THE STAGE TO COOPER'S CREEK

Carrying two passengers and money for the local bank, the stage to Cooper's Creek left Tombstone and never arrived — it just vanished. Cooper's Creek becomes the scene of shootouts, and Marshal Willard, accompanied by a young investigator, is soon headed for a deserted mining town. They find what they are looking for, except for one missing parcel. Only an old miner can tell them what happened — but can they track him down and get him to talk?

TOM BENSON

THE STAGE TO COOPER'S CREEK

Complete and Unabridged

LINFORD
Leicester

First published in Great Britain in 2006 by
Robert Hale Limited
London

First Linford Edition
published 2007
by arrangement with
Robert Hale Limited
London

British Library CIP Data

Benson, Tom, *1929 –*
    The stage to Cooper's Creek.—
    Large print ed.—
    Linford western library
    1. Stagecoach robberies—Fiction
    2. Western stories 3. Large type books
    I. Title
    823.9'2 [F]

    ISBN 978–1–84617–888–7 7902361

Published by
F. A. Thorpe (Publishing)
Anstey, Leicestershire

Set by Words & Graphics Ltd.
Anstey, Leicestershire
Printed and bound in Great Britain by
T. J. International Ltd., Padstow, Cornwall

This book is printed on acid-free paper

1

The three horses grazed mournfully on what little dry grass there was. They paid no attention to the men who lay at the top of the slope, scanning the horizon with growing impatience. It was still hot although the sun was casting longer shadows and the haze of heat was lifting enough to show the distant hills and tree line.

'It'll be dark in another couple of hours,' one of the watchers said tautly as he scratched his face. 'I reckon this friend of yours has got it all wrong or else he's playin' us for a bunch of rubes.'

The speaker was a thick-set man in his forties. He was unwashed and unshaven, with a dark face and pale eyes that were screwed up to watch the trail.

'The stage always comes through this

way,' the man on his left answered angrily. 'Alex Cullen ain't never let me down yet, and you two fellas were in on that last trick we planned. That was Alex's tip-off. And you did right well out of it. Something's gone wrong back in Silverton. Maybe they had trouble with the mules or lost a wheel.'

The third man was younger and rolled over on his side to grin good-naturedly at his companions.

'Maybe some other fella held up the stage,' he suggested.

They both looked at him but neither seemed to appreciate his attempt at humour.

'Well, they sure as hell ain't gonna be travellin' in the dark,' the thick-set man growled. 'I reckon we've wasted our time, and I don't figure to hang around here any longer.'

He started to rise to his feet but the man who had planned it all tugged at his sleeve.

'Let's give it another hour,' he suggested urgently. 'The stage has to be somewhere close by now.'

The thick-set man pulled away angrily. 'We've waited long enough,' he bawled. 'They'd have been here four, five hours ago if they was travellin' to Cooper's Creek. We've been sold a bum steer and I ain't hangin' around until some marshal shows up with a posse.' He turned to the youngest man. 'Go get the horses, Bert.'

All three were standing now and the leader scanned the horizon desperately. There was no sign of life, and even as he watched, the shadows seemed to grow longer.

'Yeah, I reckon as you might be right, Hank,' he admitted, 'but I don't figure it were Alex Cullen's fault. Somethin' has gone wrong back at the last halt.'

Young Bert bounded down the slope to tighten the girths on the horses while the other two followed him slowly. The thick-set Hank brought up the rear. His face was set hard and he gave a little nod to young Bert over the shoulder of the gang leader. Their unsuspecting boss never heard the gun being drawn from its holster. It was too late when the click of the hammer warned him of danger. Before he could turn round, a shot blasted the air and a bullet took him in the back.

He stumbled forward on his knees, rolled a few yards until almost under the hoofs of the startled animals, and then came to rest at the feet of young Bert.

'Did you have to kill him, Hank?' the young man asked quietly.

'I aim to make me a profit on this deal,' Hank said as he put away the Colt. 'This fella was all talk, and that don't buy a drink or a woman. We've got his horse and saddle, a coupla guns, and whatever cash money he's carryin' in that poke stickin' out of his vest.'

He bent down to turn over the body and remove the small leather bag by its drawstrings. It held fifteen dollars and Hank grinned happily as he put it in his own pocket.

'Billy Saunders will give us a decent price for the rest, and then we can take a little ride into a town I'm sure as hell eager to visit.'

'And what town would that be, Hank?' the young man asked.

'Cooper's Creek, fella. Where else?'

Bert's eyes blinked rapidly. 'You gotta be mad to go there,' he howled. 'We've just been tryin' to hold up their stage.'

'Bert, we ain't held up any stage and the folk in that little old gopher hole don't even know we exist. I aim to sell this stuff to Billy, and then we ride all peaceful and friendly-like to Cooper's Creek. There's a fella there who could be useful to us, one way or another: fella by the name of Alex Cullen. So saddle up, brother mine, we're out to make money.'

★ ★ ★

Cooper's Creek was no gopher hole. It was a clean little town of one main street edged with an array of stores

5

and a small bank. The creek ran with pure water and there were plenty of trees still growing along its banks. Side streets radiated wildly into a maze of alleys that led to corrals and warehouses. It was a busy place that serviced the local ranching community and the copper-mining industry. They had a newly installed telegraph and were able to boast a weekly stage that came from Tombstone via Silverton every Thursday.

But not this Thursday. Something had gone wrong and there was an anxious meeting in the office of the mayor. Aaron Stromer was a large man, prone to sweat heavily and with a red face against which his white moustache stood out like a frothy beer stain. He sat behind his desk while the marshal and the Wells Fargo agent stood before him.

'Well, that's the telegraph report,' he said grimly. 'The stage left Tombstone, called in to Silverton as usual, and left there at the regular time. It should have been here three or four hours ago. It's up to you, Ted.'

Marshal Payne's tall, lanky body was inclined to stoop and he displayed a diffident air that belied his toughness. He was known to be fair and honest and was well liked around Cooper's Creek. He shifted his weight to the other foot and made a decision.

'I'll telegraph the Silverton marshal to ride down the trail with a few fellas,' he said slowly, 'and I'll meet him somewhere along the way. If the stage has broken down or been held up, we'll find out, one way or another. I reckon that's the best way to handle it, but it might be an all-night job.'

The mayor nodded and looked at the Wells Fargo man.

'What can you tell us about it, Harry?' he asked. 'Anythin' valuable on board?'

Harry Thomas shook his head.

'Pretty normal,' he said. 'A few bits of small freight, two passengers, and some money and papers for the bank. You'd have to ask Paul Massey how much cash he was expecting, but the payroll for the copper company might be due about now, and there's a small parcel of some sort for a drillin' company. Could be a coupla thousand or more, all told.'

'Worth a hold-up then?' the mayor speculated gloomily.

'I reckon so. But not many folks know when the payroll is actually due. I don't talk none and I'm damned sure the bank don't. Moneylenders know how to keep their mouths shut.'

The conference ended a few minutes later and the marshal went across to the telegraph office to send off his message. The reply soon came and he left town an hour later with three volunteers and supplies to last the night.

* * *

They travelled north along the trail for about an hour. Then darkness set in and the little party halted and made a fire. It was not possible to go further over a trail that was not clearly marked and where signs of the missing stage would not show up until the moon was well risen in the clear sky.

They set out again at dawn after fitful sleep and a hot meal to warm them up again. They had travelled for about half an hour when one of the posse pointed to something that lay ahead. It was the body of a man.

They all dismounted and Marshal Payne examined the corpse carefully. It was nobody he knew and there was no sign of a gun or anything of value to be seen. The man had been killed by one shot in the back and had not been dead for very long. The lawman looked around but the wind had blown away any marks from wheels or horses. Ted Payne scratched his head as he stared at the hills in the far distance.

'We'll wait here,' he said after some thought. 'The Silverton fellas must be on their way, and we can see the trail clear to them hills.'

'Well, there sure as hell ain't no sign of the stage, Marshal,' one of the men said. 'Where the blazes can it be?'

Ted Payne tried to look cheerful. 'Oh, I figure as how it broke down some place and Marshal Williams has already found it. He'll probably just send one rider to join up with us and deliver the news. We may as well stay with this dead fella. After all, we gotta haul him back to town.'

'He ain't got no horse,' one of the posse pointed out.

'Yeah, I did notice that. So he'll be slung across one of your saddles.'

That was not a solution that pleased anybody and a silence fell as they set to building another fire and getting out the coffee pot.

A cloud of dust on the horizon about an hour later got the posse from Cooper's Creek to their feet. They stood watching as a group of six horsemen approached from the north. There was no sign of a stage coach and they waited impatiently as Marshal

Williams and the men from Silverton drew rein.

They had found no sign of a stage anywhere on their route. Four mules, a heavy vehicle, a guard, driver and two passengers had completely disappeared.

2

Cooper's Creek was still full of excitement. A couple of weeks had passed and the unknown man had been buried in the plot behind the meeting hall. The town was paying and so the cheapest casket was used. Nobody admitted to knowing who he was but more than half the locals trooped through the mortician's premises to view the body.

There was still no sign of the missing stage although searches had been made and the telegraph wires had never stopped humming with official messages. And now a federal officer had arrived and was installed at Ma Duncan's boarding house. He was a large man with a florid face that spoke of a liking for the bottle. A little past middle age, he was still handsome and the ladies gave him their best smiles. He wore a dark jacket and suede waistcoat that bore his badge. He had come in on a stage and hired a horse locally.

He then called a meeting of the town folk to tell them what was happening. They gathered willingly at the meeting house to listen to the news he brought. The oil lamps gave a warm glow and the moths flew around, beating their wings noisily on the glass. The federal marshal and their own lawman stood in front of the preacher's dais while the mayor and the other prominent folk sat in the front row.

Marshal Willard was a good speaker. He used a slight southern accent, and that in itself was enough to please most people.

'Now, I wanna ask you folks some questions that I reckon your own marshal may already have asked, but they gotta be repeated. Was any of you expectin' visits from a Ma Smith or a Ma Edgeton?'

He looked around without much hope as a general shaking of heads greeted his query.

'Well, they was both booked to get off here in Cooper's Creek,' he said wearily. 'Ma Smith boarded the stage at Tombstone, and Ma Edgeton got on at Silverton. Abe Lawson was the usual driver, and Will Carr was the guard.'

He looked around again in the hope of some response. There was none.

'Well, that's the way things are,' he said in a discouraged voice. 'And I'd sure welcome any ideas you folks might have.'

His eye had caught a tall man who stood near the door. The man was young and lean, with pale features and a wide mouth. He looked to be in his twenties and was dressed in much the same way as the federal man. He carried a gun and leaned against the wall in a posture that reminded Marshal Willard of an actor playing a part. Playing the part of a professional gun, but not doing it very successfully.

There were two other strangers in the hall as well, but they were just ordinary cowpokes and did not stand out from the crowd. One was the thickset Hank, and the other was his brother, Bert. They stood at the back, lounging against the wall and listening to what was being said with mild interest.

They had sold all the belongings of the man Hank had shot and now had a few dollars to spend. They arrived in Cooper's Creek a few days ago, and were looking around discreetly for Alex Cullen.

The two of them retired to the Golden Horse saloon when the meeting broke up. They intended to have a few more drinks and listen to the talk among the locals. Somebody must eventually mention the name of Cullen and set them on the right path. They had checked every store sign and looked for initials branded on horses or saddles. Nothing had given them a clue and the two men were beginning to get a little desperate.

'They gotta hell of a lotta law in this town, Hank,' young Bert said anxiously as they sipped their beer. 'That federal fella and the local marshal will be checkin' on every stranger in the place. And there's a deputy hangin' around as well. I figure as how we should get the hell outa Cooper's Creek.

Hank grinned. 'Look, Bert,' he said in a low voice, 'we're just a coupla cowpokes lookin' for work. We ain't known here and we're not on any wanted list. When we find this Cullen fella, he can put us on to another job someplace.'

'Suppose he don't want to work with us?'

Hank shrugged his shoulders. 'We could tell tales to the law. Or we could kill him. He ain't got a choice. Besides, if he helps us the way he must have helped Al Mortimer, he'll be gettin' a share of the take.'

Hank looked round the saloon. It was beginning to fill up as more men came in from the meeting. They were still talking about it and the noise grew as the place got busier. Hank suddenly put down his glass with enough force to spill some of the beer.

'I bin a right fool,' he said in a hoarse whisper. 'Who's the fella in a town who knows everybody from birth to death?'

Bert thought it over. His eyes wrinkled as he tried to fathom what his brother was getting at.

'Who would that be, Hank?' he asked after a pause.

'The doctor. That's who. We all end up in front of these medical fellas sooner or later. I reckon that's the man we gotta talk to.'

Bert thought it over. 'But will he tell us?' he asked. 'Them medicos ain't talkative. I'm told they got some sorta code.'

His brother looked at him as if not believing that Bert could possibly come up with anything sensible.

'You could be right,' he said grudgingly. 'But there's another fella we can try. There was a preacher in that meetin' tonight. We could pay him a visit.'

'Do we have to go a-prayin' and hymn singing?' Bert asked nervously.

'No, nothin' that serious. We just go along and tell him we're lookin' for ranch work and was told that a fella called Alex Cullen might be able to help us. Let's go.'

'At this time of night, Hank? He'll be abed.'

The older man looked at his brother pityingly.

'He was at the meetin' alongside the lawmen,' he explained patiently, 'and he'll be tidyin' up the place now that all the folks have gone. If we stir our butts, we'll catch him before he heads for home.'

He put down his glass and made for the door. Bert quickly swallowed his beer and followed anxiously. They went back down the street and entered the open door of the meeting house. The preacher was standing on a chair dousing the various oil lamps. The place was already in semi-darkness and he peered short-sightedly at the two men

18

who confronted him.

The Reverend Eli Warren was a small man with a black suit that seemed too big for his thin frame. His face was ruddy, but lined and topped by a halo of grey hair. His glasses were perched on the end of a beaky nose and his general expression was one of rather bewildered benevolence.

He listened carefully as Hank explained what they wanted. His eyes flickered as the name of Alex Cullen was mentioned.

'I do not recall a man of that name in Cooper's Creek,' he said with a rather quavery precision. 'You must have got it wrong someways. And as to getting ranch work at this time of the year, I think it rather unlikely. The drives are over and hands are being laid off. I'm sorry I can't be of help.'

The two brothers left the meeting house and Bert trailed behind Hank as they headed back to the saloon.

'What do we do now?' he asked as they entered the building. 'That weren't no help, no how.'

His brother grinned, and instead of going over to the bar, he stood by the window and peered into the dark street.

'You got a touchin' faith in folks that I don't have,' he said quietly. 'That preacher fella was lookin' mighty uncomfortable when he told us there ain't no Alex Cullen. Many a man's been hanged for lookin' less guilty. He knew somethin' that he didn't want to pass on, brother mine. I aim to see what he does next.'

Bert was sent to fetch a couple of beers while his brother stared through the glass in the direction of the meeting house. He let out a little gasp of satisfaction when the windows of the place darkened completely as the preacher doused the last of the lamps. A figure appeared in the doorway a short time later and Hank hurriedly put down the newly acquired beer glass on the nearest table. He strode from the saloon, and Bert had to follow.

The preacher crossed the street and

entered an alley between a couple of closed stores. The two men followed at a distance and were just in time to see him turn right at the end of the narrow lane. There were corrals there and an old shed with no roof. The little man groped his way along the wooden walls of two buildings until he came to the door he wanted. He knocked urgently and Hank watched from the corner.

The door opened and a patch of light flooded out for a moment. The preacher entered and the door closed again. Hank made his way quietly along the board walk and looked at the building and at those on either side of it. He motioned his brother to go quietly back the way they had come. As they reached the street again, Hank let out a grunt of triumph.

'Well, if that don't beat the hell outa all,' he chuckled. 'That preacher fella has just gone in the back door of the saloon.'

Bert thought it over for a moment and did not speak until they reached the front of the Golden Horse.

'Maybe he likes a drop to drink,' he suggested. 'Some of them preacher fellas ain't keen to let folks see them at a bar.'

'Bert, you've got it all wrong. That preacher has gone to warn somebody that we're askin' about Alex Cullen. Now, let's go back in there and see if the fella what runs the place is anywhere around.'

Their eyes blinked under the bright lights as they ordered more beer. Hank leaned across as the barman served it.

'Ever heard tell of a fella called Alex Cullen?' he asked quietly.

The man shook his head. 'Can't say that I have,' he said without interest.

'Who owns this place?' Hank asked with a slight edge to his voice.

The barman nodded to the other side of the saloon. He was indicating a short man who sat at one of the tables talking to a couple of others who had been playing cards. They were chatting like old friends and seemed wrapped in each other's company.

'That's Fred Siddons,' the bartender said. 'He started this place up nigh on thirty years ago. Wants to sell if you've got the sort of money he's askin' for it. Him and his wife is gettin' on in years now and I reckon as how they've had enough of saloons.'

Hank thought it over for a moment or two. 'I just saw the preacher go in your back door,' he said tentatively. 'Likes to take a quiet drink, does he?'

The barman grinned. 'He ain't a drinkin' man, but we got a few girls upstairs. They give a fella a good time for a dollar or less. Just go round back and knock the way he did. You'll have a good night.'

Hank glanced at his grinning brother. 'I might just do that,' he said without conviction.

None of them knew that the preacher was back on the street before the two brothers even reached the front door of the saloon. He had delivered his message and gone scurrying home to his ailing and complaining wife.

'I think we're wastin' our time here, Hank,' Bert said anxiously. 'Why not get the hell outa this town before some of these folks start gettin' interested in us?'

The older brother thought about it for a moment and then slowly nodded his head. He was not going to admit that Bert could be having a good idea.

'I bin thinkin' about that,' he said smugly, 'but we ain't quittin' without makin' a profit from this one-eyed hole. There's a gun store down the street, and the owner is right over there at the end of the bar. He's talkin' to that big fella, and the store's empty. There weren't no lights on when we passed it and I heard tell that his wife is dead and his son is workin' outa town. If we go in the back door, we can have ourselves a few guns and be outa town without causin' any fuss. Are you game for it?'

Bert nodded. The idea of action was much easier than any more thinking.

'Sure am,' he said happily.

'Then go saddle our horses and walk them round behind the store. It's a narrow alley and dark as hell. I'll join you there in about twenty minutes.'

'Why ain't you comin' to help me with the horses?'

'I wanta make sure the storekeeper doesn't take off before we're ready. Bring the horses past this place, and when I see you on the street, I'll finish my drink and just walk outa here like a fella goin' to his bed. Now, move it, brother mine, and empty everythin' out of the saddlebags that we don't need. I aim to fill them with somethin' more valuable.'

Bert nodded and left the saloon. His brother stayed at the bar, sipping peacefully and watching the storekeeper who was drinking whiskey and holding forth in an ever-louder voice.

Hank could catch a glimpse of the street through the mirror that dominated the bar. The windows were misted a little but anybody going past with two horses would be easily seen.

He waited patiently until the figure of Bert appeared leading the two animals. Hank turned to get a better view through the steamed-up window. There was no doubt that it was his brother who was passing, and the younger man jerked his head nervously as he neared the Golden Horse. Hank smiled to himself, finished his drink, and strolled slowly out into the night.

He moved down the street among the few locals, and turned into the alley between the gun store and a drapery store. The alley was rutted and dark. It stank of horses, and as he reached the far end, a line of small corrals and privies could be seen against the sky. Their own animals stood tied to a rail and Bert was sheltering under the rear porch of the gun store.

Hank joined him, and after looking round carefully, he examined the door with keen attention.

'It's locked tight and I reckon there's bolts top and bottom,' he said quietly.

He looked at the window next to the

door. It was barred and there were wooden shutters behind the glass. The place was well guarded.

'How the hell do we get in?' Bert asked hoarsely.

'I'll give it a good bootin' round the lock and the bottom bolt. The top one will be easy work.'

Bert took fright. 'That will make one hell of a noise,' he protested.

'Usually does, but you'll be at the other end of the town openin' the gates of them corrals behind the livery stable. With a mass of horses and mules chargin' into the main street, folk ain't gonna be payin' attention to what I'm doin' here. Now get down there and use a bit of whoopin' and hollerin' to liven the place up.'

He patted his brother on the shoulder and the two men exchanged grins in the darkness. Bert set off while Hank waited patiently for the ruckus that would follow when the animals were turned loose among the late revellers.

He was soon rewarded. There were shouts in the distance, then a flurry of hoofs. He could see people running on the main street as he peered round the corner of the alley.

Hank grinned as he stood back from the door and raised his right foot. The thud against the lock area seemed to vibrate in the darkness. He felt, rather than heard, the splintering of the wood as he booted the lower section of the door. It gave way and he could hear part of the bolt falling off inside the building. He heaved his shoulder against the woodwork and the door flew open and banged loudly against the wall of the hallway.

Hank let out a triumphal gasp and entered the gun store. He heard two distinct clicks as he moved forward. It was all over in a second as the shotgun blasts caught him and he stumbled backwards onto the porch with his chest and face blown away.

3

The lawman had to push his way through the excited crowd. There were lights on now in the gun store and the owner was standing at the side of a young lad who trembled in the night air and still clutched a shotgun in his shaking hands. Hank lay in a large pool of blood that was dripping off the stoop to be trodden underfoot by the mob of eager townsfolk.

Marshal Payne looked at the body and then turned to the owner for an explanation. Jack Mead had run the gun store for nearly twenty years and was a short, stout man with long sideburns and a wide, full-lipped mouth. He was known to be fond of his drink and his face was now flushed as he explained.

'Tim here was sleepin' down behind the counter, Marshal,' he said. 'He always stays over if I want an hour or two out now and then. I don't like to leave a place like this empty, and Tim's a good, reliable lad. Ain't that right, fella?'

He put a comradely arm around the lad's shoulder and the lawman noticed the young fellow wince slightly.

'Suppose you tell me what happened, Tim?' Ted Payne said quietly.

'I was hunkered down behind the counter, just like Mr Mead told you,' the youth said tremulously. 'I'd gone off to sleep, I had, when there's one almighty bangin' at the back door. Real shook the building, it did. I grabbed the shotgun and went to see what was happenin' there. The door suddenly bursts wide open and this fella is in the store. I just fired blind, Marshal. It was as scary as hell, it was.'

Ted Payne nodded understandingly. 'I can imagine, lad,' he said kindly, 'but you did the right thing. So don't go frettin' about it.' He turned to the crowd. 'Anybody know who this dead fella is?'

There was a jostling as they all tried to peer closer at the corpse.

'I figure as how he was in the Golden Horse a short time back,' somebody shouted. 'It ain't easy to say, but he looks like a fella who was with a younger stranger. They been in town for a few days now.'

Ted Payne looked round for any more help and a few of the men seemed to agree.

'So where's this other fella?' he asked. 'And who the hell let all them horses outa the corrals?'

Nobody knew the answer to that and they could all hear the commotion on the main street as the animals were still being rounded up and herded back to the corrals. The federal marshal had now joined the group and the mayor was pushing his way busily through the mob. He recoiled slightly when he saw the body and made sure that he did not tread in the blood.

'This lad has done a good job,' he said in his best vote-catching voice.

'He's saved us a trial and made the town a safer place. So now let's all go to our homes, folks. The marshal here is in control of the situation and we can all sleep peaceable in our beds.'

The crowd did not want to go home. What with a stampede and a shooting, it was promising to be a good night. They milled around while the mortician took charge of Hank's body and the more important people moved into the gun store and closed what was left of the back door behind them. Marshal Payne had spoken to his deputy and sent him hurrying to the main street.

The living quarters of the store were warm and a slight smell of burnt powder clung to the air. Young Tim put on the coffee while the two marshals and the mayor shared the whiskey bottle that Jack Mead happily produced. The lad was now over his intial shock and beginning to realise that he was the town hero. His hands were steady as he poured the coffee and listened to his elders discussing events.

'I've sent Mel Ridley to take a look round the town and see where this other fella is,' the marshal said as they drank. 'Some of the folks will go with him in case he needs help, and maybe we'll find what the hell's been goin' on.'

'I reckon the animals was set loose all deliberate,' the mayor put in eagerly. 'Then they could break into this place under cover of all the noise. It's a good thing young Tim was here. And them two horses tied to the rail back there. They tell us all we need to know. The other fella's on foot now.'

'Unless he can steal another horse,' the federal marshal said drily.

'But he ain't got a saddle,' the mayor pointed out. 'I reckon we'll have him in no time.'

'I'll go and scout round myself,' Ted Payne said when he had finished his drink. 'We've got their horses so at least the town's made some profit outa the mess.'

'Will it pay for my door?' Jack Mead asked eagerly.

'Ask the mayor,' the marshal grinned as he and the federal man headed for the street.

Young Bert had already been located, but his finder was quietly watching events for the moment. The tall young man who had stood at the back of the meeting hall had not lost sight of the two brothers. He had watched them go to the saloon, then back to the meeting house. And he had chosen to follow Bert when he went to saddle up the horses and leave them with his brother behind the store.

The watcher had smiled slightly as he saw the corral gates being opened and all the animals being waved to freedom. He guessed what sort of game the two men were playing, and followed Bert as he hurried back to the store.

The shots took both of them by surprise. Bert was only a few yards from the rear door of the gun store. He stopped in his tracks and stared in horror as his brother suddenly appeared and fell backwards onto the stoop. The watcher was on the corner of the alley and could not see what had happened. He was not prepared for the sudden dash as young Bert hurtled past him towards the maze of corrals and huts where he might find some safety.

People began to arrive and the tall man quietly joined them. He saw Hank's body and viewed it without any show of emotion. Then he left the crowd and walked back slowly in the direction taken by young Bert. Lights were going on and the darkness was lifting as he reached a row of corrals and a hut that housed fodder for the animals. He put his ear against the flimsy planking of the wall and listened for a moment or two. He could hear a slight movement in the darkness as though somebody was moving bales of straw about. The man smiled and moved on.

The main street was still crowded with excited people. The town marshal, his deputy, and practically everybody else moved restlessly in a search for the companion of the dead man. The young watcher crossed to tap Marshal Payne on the arm.

'I saw a fella go into that hut by the row of corrals back there,' he said urgently as he pointed down the alley from which he had just emerged.

The lawman needed no second telling. He headed for the fodder store followed by the crowd. The young man trailed behind as though trying to distance himself from what was happening. The federal marshal was at Ted Payne's side while the deputy, at the other end of the street, saw the general movement and hurried to join them.

A few people were carrying lanterns that helped to illuminate the scene. Lights shone in some rear windows and the old plank door of the fodder shed could be seen swaying gently on its hinges. A keen, cool wind moved it with a slight squeak as the marshal took out his pistol while he pulled the door wide open and motioned everybody else to stand back.

'If you're in there, fella,' he shouted, 'you'd better come out all quiet-like. I ain't got much patience but I sure got plenty of fire-power.'

The crowd fell silent as they waited avidly for what would happen next.

'I'm comin' out,' a voice called meekly.

They could hear movements in the shed and then the figure of Bert appeared in the doorway. His hands were in the air and he carried no gun. His holster was empty.

'That's the fella,' somebody shouted. 'I saw him in the saloon with the other one.'

The deputy passed them, carrying a lantern he had borrowed. He entered the shed and came back a moment or two later with Bert's .44 Colt. A little procession now walked in the direction of the jailhouse.

Once the prisoner was safely inside, the mayor and the lawmen spoke to the crowd to try and disperse them. Excitement was still high and some of the men headed determinedly for the saloon. Fred Siddons was standing at the door of the Golden Horse with his wife at his side. They had not wanted to miss any of the fun but Fred now decided to lock up for the night and seek his bed. Ma Siddons was made of sterner stuff.

'Don't be such a mugwump,' she snapped. 'There'll be folks on the street for the next hour, and they'll all be in need of a drink. If we aim to retire in the next year or two, we need to take this town for every cent we can.'

Ma Siddons spoke good sense, and her stout, well-built body in beige bombazine glided back inside to order the bar staff to get ready for another rush. Fred followed meekly, dominated by her as usual but knowing that it made good sense.

Bert was safely in a cell and the lamps gave a warm glow to the marshal's office. The mayor lingered while the federal man and Ted Payne looked through the bars at their new prisoner.

'Suppose you tell us all about yourself and your friend,' Ted Payne suggested.

'Ain't nothin' to tell,' Bert answered sulkily. 'I ain't done nothin' wrong.'

'Is that a fact now? Then who let all the animals outa the corrals while your partner smashed in the back door of the gun store? You tellin' me that you was just takin' a quiet drink some place while all that was happenin' in the town?'

'We was drunk, Marshal. Just drunk.'

'Were you now? So what are you doin' in Cooper's Creek?'

There was a silence and the two lawmen looked at each other. Ted Payne went across to the bars of the cell, put one large hand through, and grabbed Bert by the front of his shirt. He pulled the young fellow until his frightened face was pressed against the rough metal.

'If I have to come into that cell, lad,'

the lawman said quietly, 'and damage my fists while I'm beatin' the hell outa you, that'll make me real mad. I like to keep my hands all nice and smooth for my crocheting. Understand me?'

Bert gulped noisily. 'Yes, Marshal,' he muttered.

'So start talkin' while you still have some teeth.'

He released his hold on the young man and stood back to listen. The mayor tried to look shocked at the marshal's attitude but was also engaged in opening a bottle of whiskey he had found in the drawer of the desk.

Bert leaned against the bars, his hands holding on to them as though they were supporting him.

'Hank and me is brothers,' he said slowly. 'Hank and Bert Blansky. We ain't done nothin' real bad, Marshal. Just a bit of thievin' here and there. We came to town lookin' for an easy mark, and saw the gun store fella gettin' drunk in the saloon. So Hank said to let out the horses while he burst into the

40

store. And it all went wrong.'

'It sure did. You'll do a spell in federal prison, fella.'

Marshal Willard had listened silently, and he now glanced at the local lawman.

'Can I ask him something?'

'Sure, go ahead,' Ted Payne urged him cheerfully.

The federal man approached the bars until he was only a foot or two away from Bert.

'Who's Alex Cullen?' he asked quietly. 'you've been makin' enquiries about him all over town.'

The young man's face changed expression. He opened his mouth to deny everything but saw the looks on the faces of his captors.

'He's a fella in town who can give us information on jobs,' he said in a small voice.

'There ain't no fella in Cooper's Creek by that name,' the mayor piped up firmly.

'We found that out. All the folks we

asked said they'd never heard tell of him,' Bert agreed eagerly. 'So we decided to pull the store job and then leave town.'

'Who told you about this Alex Cullen?' the federal marshal asked.

Bert blinked rapidly. 'It were Hank as was told. I don't know nothin' about it.'

Marshal Payne joined the federal man at the cell bars.

'What do you know about the missin' stage?' he asked grimly. The prisoner shook his head. 'Nothin' at all, Marshal,' he protested. 'It never turned up.'

There was a silence in the jailhouse as the two lawmen looked at each other and the mayor stood with a glass halfway to his lips.

'So you and your brother was waitin' to rob the stage,' Ted Payne said slowly.

The prisoner looked as though he would deny it for a moment or two, but then had second thoughts.

'We never even saw it,' he answered quietly. 'Waited for hours, we did. This

Alex Cullen fella had tipped off . . . '

He stopped in mid-flow as he recalled the unidentified corpse and the cheap burial. ' . . . had tipped off my brother,' he finished weakly.

'Had he tipped off your brother to any other jobs?' Ted Payne asked.

'No.'

'So, tell me, lad,' the marshal asked as he approached the bars menacingly. 'How come your brother didn't know who the fella was and had to search Cooper's Creek for him?'

There was a silence and Bert Blansky stared round the jailhouse as though looking for inspiration.

'You're lyin' like hell, lad,' Ted Payne said grimly as he crossed to the desk to pick up the keys, 'so I reckon as how I have to come in there and beat it outa you.'

Before he could do any more, the jailhouse door opened violently and Mel Ridley, his deputy, came breathlessly into the office.

'We got trouble, Marshal,' he gasped.

'The folk over in the Golden Horse are real liquored-up and they're figurin' on lynchin' this hombre. They reckon as how him and the other fella have somethin' to do with the stage vanishing. They're real mad and talkin' about them two women passengers bein' killed. We gotta stop them, Marshal.'

The mayor paled and went over to the window to look down the street. The saloon was well lit and people were gathered outside it. He could hear the noise and started calculating whether to leave by the front or the back of the building.

The two marshals opened the jailhouse door and went to stand out on the stoop. They were seen by the gathering mob in front of the saloon and the noise grew as more people came to join them. There were few women about. It was too late for them to be on the street.

'You'd better calm them down,' the mayor urged Marshal Payne. 'Tell them to leave it to the law and go home.'

The marshal looked undecided and glanced at his federal colleague and the deputy. All he saw were worried faces as the drinkers began to pour cut of the saloon and some of the town trouble-makers started haranguing them. The federal man shook his head despairingly and put a hand on the marshal's arm.

'This looks bad, and we either have to arm ourselves or just lock up the jailhouse and leave quietly. Whichever we do, there's gonna be killing.'

'And I'd rather it was the fella in there that was killed than any of the townsfolk — or us,' the mayor quavered. 'Let's get the hell outa here while we still can. I've seen lynch mobs before.'

Marshal Payne noticed that his deputy had already vanished. He looked at the mob and saw that several of them were carrying ropes and waving them drunkenly around. He knew that a few shotgun blasts might be effective, but they were his neighbours, and he hated to do it.

'We'll lock up the jailhouse and leave by the back,' he said quietly. 'I don't aim to kill folks I've known all my days. Not for the scum we've got back in the cell there.'

'Now you're talking,' the mayor breathed thankfully.

They hurried back inside and locked the front door as some sort of token gesture. Then the three men passed their prisoner and left by the rear door. The marshal locked it behind him and put the key in his pocket as a symbol of securing his office and doing his duty.

The mob were already smashing the windows and somebody had run round to the smithy for a large hammer. The door soon splintered and gave way to admit a crowd that filled the small place. They stared for a moment at the terrified man behind the bars and then somebody spotted the keys on the desk and waved them triumphantly. Bert was dragged out, shouting and begging for mercy. They hustled him down the street to the livery stable and flung a rope up over the loading beam. Bert's struggles were useless as a noose was placed round his neck and several men got ready to haul him off his feet.

The shot took them all by surprise.

There was a stunned silence as the tautening rope snapped in a ragged mess and Bert, already on his toes, fell to the ground. The mob turned to look at the solitary figure of a tall young man in dark clothes. He held a shotgun in his hands and stood silently in the middle of the street.

The blacksmith was the first to recover his poise.

'You gotta be one fool fella, mister,' he shouted. 'We got room for another one up there.'

The young man raised the gun slightly.

'And I got another load of shot,' he said quietly. 'And then a Colt that will kill a few more of you. Take this fella back to the jailhouse and lock him up.'

There was a muttering but nobody moved towards him.

'Why should we?' somebody shouted from a safe position.

'You're hangin' this fella because you think he has somethin' to do with four missin' people and a stage coach. Am I right?'

There was a nodding of heads.

'You got the right of it there, fella,' one of the store owners said with sudden sanity.

'Then how the hell are you gonna find out what happened once he's dead?'

There was a long silence and then the blacksmith began to remove the remnants of the noose from Bert's sore neck. The mob marched him slowly back to the jailhouse.

4

The jailhouse was warm and one of the oil lamps smoked a little to add to the smell of sweat and coffee. The mayor had scurried off home as soon as trouble began but the two marshals returned when they realised that one young man had controlled the whole angry town.

He sat at the other side of the lawman's desk now, his face pale under the light and a slightly uneasy grin around his mouth. Bert Blansky was back in the cell, lying on the bunk and still shivering at his narrow brush with death. He could not sleep and listened listlessly to what the others were saying.

The two marshals looked a little sheepish as they held their coffee mugs and viewed the stranger with embarrassed interest.

'You did a good job back there, fella,'

Ted Payne admitted, 'but you sure took one hell of a risk. So tell us who you are and why you interfered.'

The young stranger put down his own mug and leaned forward on the bentwood chair.

'My name's Bill Pearce, Marshal,' he said quietly. 'I'm employed by the Nathaniel Copper Company to do a little investigatin' for them.'

The federal man snorted. 'A Pinkerton fella,' he groaned. 'That's all we need right now.'

'No, no. I'm not a Pinkerton agent. I tried to get a job with them but they turned me down. Said I hadn't enough experience. I work for myself and the copper company hired me over this stage business. They got an interest in it.'

'And what would that be?' Marshall Payne asked.

Bill Pearce grinned. 'These copper-minin' fellas is real mean, Marshal,' he said. 'They didn't hire the Pinkertons because it cost too much. I was doin' odd jobs in Tombstone and they heard about one that had worked out well. They took me on at about half what it would have cost to use the big timers. I work real cheap. I got to.'

Marshal Willard nodded as though he understood.

'I saw you back at the meetin' house,' he said. 'You looked to me like you was some actor-fella playin' the part of a gunfighter. Dressed right, walked right, but as green as fresh grass. You ever shot anybody, son?'

The young man shook his head. 'Never have, Marshal,' he admitted.

'I reckoned not. You've got one hell of a nerve though. So why did these fellas hire you?'

'Well, the copper company have got some new drills they're usin' out at Mesa Falls. They're supposed to go through rock like it was cheese. And they're driven by diamonds.'

'Diamonds!'

Ted Payne nearly fell out of his chair and Bert Blansky sat upright in his cell.

Only Marshal Willard remained cool.

'I've heard tell of diamond drills,' he said. 'Industrial diamonds is what they're called. They've been usin' them back east, and the big gold-minin' companies are tryin' them out up north of here. They ain't anythin' like the diamonds the womenfolk wear. Just bits of rough stone that are hard enough to cut through rock.'

'Are they valuable?' Marshal Payne asked.

The federal man shrugged and looked to Bill Pearce for guidance.

'Well, that's the tricky thing,' he said. 'The company was shippin' out some of these diamonds to Mesa Falls and they was worth about two thousand dollars. It was just a small package but Wells Fargo would have charged them dependin' on the value. They don't look nothin' so the copper-minin' fellas just said that it was gravel samples bein' freighted. Cost practically nothin' to carry on the stage and they'd used the trick a few times before. But it all went wrong now, and they're mad as hell. They can't claim from Wells Fargo and they can't claim on their insurance. So they hired me.'

'So what have you found out?' It was Marshal Willard who asked and his voice was sharp.

'I checked around Tombstone before goin' on to Silverton,' Bill Pearce said eagerly, 'but there weren't no leads in either place. So I came here to see why two passengers booked to get off at Cooper's Creek. Them two fellas was already in town and askin' questions about this Alex Cullen. I watched and figured as how they'd better be kept alive until a few questions could be asked of them.'

'Yeah, and I still got some things to ask this fella,' Ted Payne said as he looked menacingly at the man in the cell. 'We was interrupted last time we was havin' a quiet talk with young Bert here.'

The marshal stood up, took the cell keys from the desk and lumbered slowly over to the bars. Bert Blansky sat up in alarm as the lawman neared him.

'You gonna tell me the rest of the tale or do I come in and hammer it outa you?'

Bert got slowly off the bunk and came over to the bars.

'It were all Hank's doin',' he said. 'We'd worked with Al Mortimer a few times and Al got his information from this Alex Cullen. When the stage didn't turn up, Hank got mad and shot Al. Swore he aimed to make a few dollars after all the sweat. Then he said we had to come into town and find this Cullen fella so that he could work with us. Hank was always quick to fly off and let loose. That's why I'm in this mess now. But he was my brother, Marshal, and the only kin I had.'

'Well, that seems to settle that side of things,' Marshal Willard said as Ted Payne walked back to the desk. 'But we still gotta find a stage and four missin' people. Any ideas, young fella?'

The two lawmen looked at Bill

Pearce, but he shook his head.

'I got no ideas,' he admitted, 'but there is somethin' that might have a bearin' on all this. I came across another fella in Silverton. He was askin' around and seemed one hell of a tough character. Never did find out who he was, and I gotta be honest and say that I wasn't anxious to cross his path. He looked real nasty.'

The lawmen glanced at each other a little uneasily.

'You ain't seen him in Cooper's Creek?' Ted Payne asked.

'No. Marshal.'

Before anything more could be said, the door slowly opened and the little preacher seemed to slide into the office. He stood sheepishly in front of the two lawmen and looked uncertainly from one to the other.

'Well, Eli,' Ted Payne said helpfully. 'Just spit it out. You ain't usually short on words.'

'I have a confession to make, Ted,' the little man admitted shakily. 'I might have done a terrible thing.'

'You didn't hold up a stage?' Marshal Willard suggested with a slight smile.

'It isn't a joking matter,' the preacher squeaked. 'This young man you have in the cells came to see me with the man who was killed robbing the gun store. They wanted to know where they could find Alex Cullen.'

'You're tellin' us nothin' new, Eli,' Ted Payne said wearily. 'We know all about that.'

'But it's what happened next. I don't know why two strangers should be so curious about Alex, but I told them I'd never heard the name. I don't like telling lies. It's not my nature, but I was just being careful. Then one of the men was killed and you arrested this one. I got nervous. And when the folks tried to lynch him, I thought it best to tell you what they'd been asking.'

'Well, we know the reason they was asking,' Ted Payne said soothingly, 'so you ain't got nothin' to worry about there. However, we'd like to know who

Alex Cullen is. It's the most important question we could ask just now.'

'Other than what happened to the stage,' Marshal Willard said softly.

'Yeah, other than that. Who is Alex Cullen?'

Eli Warren told them and the town marshal's mouth fell open in dull surprise. There was a stillness in the office for a short time while the words sank home.

'Well, if that don't beat all,' Ted Payne said softly. 'And yet I suppose it makes sense when you come to think of it. Thank you, Eli. I reckon you've just saved this town from a lotta trouble and maybe spared a few lives just for good measure.'

5

Bill Pearce was riding out of town. He had no more interest in Cooper's Creek. The stage had never reached there, the informer's identity was not his concern, and he had plans of his own. Bill was new at the business of investigating, but he had intelligence and had supplied himself with a map of the area. It was one issued by the railroad company to advertise their routes.

He had reasoned things out. If the stage never arrived at the point where the hold-up men lay in wait, then it had to turn off to some place that could be reached in reasonable time. Mules must be fed and watered. They had to be rested. The same applied to whoever was with the stage. He reckoned that a further fifteen or twenty miles would be the limit of travel, and then there had to be food and water for all concerned. He had checked the map and spotted a tiny town that stood by a small tributary of the Gila. It was a dead and alive place with no stage, no telegraph, and only surviving because it had once been the centre of a small gold find.

Bill decided that it was the first lead to try and he was heading south-west to find the run-down place. He rode with an air of confidence that he did not really feel, and hoped that whoever he met would not suss him out the way the federal marshal had done so easily.

He spent the night by a muddy creek where his horse stamped the water into an undrinkable mess. Bill slept fitfully but was able to shoot a jackrabbit for breakfast. He skinned it carefully and roasted two of the legs over the fire. The rest was left for the predators that would descend on the spot as soon as horse and rider had departed.

He moved on at an easy pace, and after breasting a long slope, the town of Fremont lay below him. It was one wide, sandy street with adobe and wooden buildings in an unsightly mix on either side. There were a few corrals and he could see some old mine workings along the narrow creek that fed the place with water. There were few people about and when he reached the north end of the street, he could see that some of the stores were closed up and the saloon was a worn place that looked as if the windows had not been cleaned for months. It advertised itself optimistically as the Golden Nugget.

There was a marshal's office, but that was also locked up, and next to it was a general store where a few women chatted. They eyed Bill without interest as he rode past. He stopped at the saloon and hitched his horse to the rail. There was only a small cow pony to keep it company and the two animals eyed each other gloomily.

The saloon was cleaner than it looked from outside and there were only three middle-aged men sitting at one table with beer in front of them.

They talked in low voices and looked up at the entry of a stranger. The bartender seemed to be a Mexican. He was short and swarthy with an easy smile at the prospect of a new face.

Bill took a beer and leaned on the counter while he sipped it. The drink was warm but tasted better than he had expected. He drank thankfully and watched the bartender drying some large glasses with a reasonably clean cloth.

'Anywhere around here I can buy a mule?' Bill asked in as casual a voice as he could muster.

The man nodded. 'George Brent, just behind the livery stable,' he said cheerfully. 'He's the only animal dealer we got, fella.'

Although looking like someone from the other side of the border, the man sounded as though he had been born and bred locally.

'I see the marshal's office is closed,' Bill went on. 'Is he anywhere around town?'

'We ain't got no marshal. Not since old Fred got thrown from his horse and went all funny. This town don't need no law. Folks just take care of their own troubles.'

'Sounds pretty good. No lawyers to upset things.'

The bartender nodded vigorously. 'We ran the judge outa town three years back,' he said. 'And Lawyer Fawcett took the hint and left soon after.'

Bill grinned. 'What about the mayor?' he asked.

'Oh, we kept him. He's the horse doctor, and he ain't a bad sorta fella. He don't steal as much as the last one. We hanged him.'

'Sounds a nice town.'

'Peaceable, fella. Real peaceable. You ain't a lawman, are you?'

'No. Just a fella what wants to buy a mule.'

'Well, George Brent's your man. But don't tangle with him. He ain't got the sweetest of tempers.'

'Neither have I.'

Bill Pearce left the saloon and walked down the street until he reached the livery stable. It was open for business but looked as woebegone as the rest of the town. A narrow alley led to a few corrals at the rear where a dilapidated shed displayed the name of George Brent as a horse dealer. There were two bedraggled cow ponies in the corral at the side of the shed. They were kept company by a single mule and Bill went over to lean across the rough fencing.

The mule bore a brand that was unreadable. It had certainly been altered and covered with paint or dirt to mask its uncertainty. Bill knew the brand he was looking for but it was not possible to say for sure what the original mark had been. The mule came over to where he stood and he leaned across to scratch its neck. It seemed grateful for a change to the monotony and stood quietly as he examined it for harness marks. There were plenty of them and it had certainly pulled some sort of heavy rig.

'You want something, fella?' The voice was a harsh one and Bill turned to find himself facing a man who had come out of the shed. He was large and had grey hair that matched the stubble around his chin. There was a scar across one eye and his belly stood out in an almost belligerent fashion of its own. He carried a gun at his side and his hand was within inches of the butt.

'I'm lookin' for a mule,' Bill said quietly. He had intended to be more direct, but the presence of this tough-looking horse dealer had made him more cautious.

'I only got the one but I can do it at a good price.'

Bill pointed to the damaged brand.

'I ain't too sure about that,' he said reluctantly. 'Looks like it's been altered recently.'

'That happens all the time in this business,' the man said dismissively. 'Animals change hands and folks like to put their own brand on 'em. It all figures in the price. I ain't askin' the earth. You interested?'

'Maybe we can do a deal. Suppose I pay you the askin' price for this mule and then walk away without him. Interested?'

George Brent looked puzzled for a moment. Then he grinned to show a row of yellowish teeth.

'You sound like a fella what wants to buy information,' he said slowly. 'If I went talkin' to strange men, folks wouldn't trust me no more. That could be bad for business.'

He came closer to the young man and looked around to make sure that nobody could overhear what was said.

'What exactly do you want to know?' he asked.

'I'm lookin' for someone who might have had four mules to sell in the past few weeks. They all had the Ed Tilson brand on them and had been pullin' a large rig.'

'Stolen?'

'I reckon so.'

George Brent scratched his chin

noisily. 'Then you'd be some sorta lawman?' he suggested.

'No, I just got an interest.'

The horse dealer moved over to the corral and leaned against the fence with his back to Bill. He stayed in that position for a full minute or so before turning round with a big grin on his face.

'It'll cost you sixty dollars,' he said.

'I said I'd pay the price of one mule, fella. Not the price of a troop of cavalry. Twenty dollars. I ain't got no more.'

'Then go finish your lessons in the school house,' George Brent sneered as he turned away. 'I know a punk kid when I see one, and I'll lay odds you never drew that gun for anythin' other than shootin' at jackrabbits.'

Bill bit his lip angrily. The man had called his bluff and he felt that he had made a complete mess of things.

'The next fella that asks about them mules won't offer a deal like I did,' he said without thinking.

George Brent swung round, letting

out a curse as he went for his gun. Bill suddenly realized that his suspicions had been right. This was the man who had done the deal. His reaction was automatic. His hand fell to the butt of the Colt and both men drew at almost the same time. It was Bill who pulled the trigger first and the big man reeled back against the wall of the shed.

He seemed to recover for a moment and tried to raise his own gun. It fell from his grip as he sank to the ground and quivered for a moment or so.

People began to arrive on the scene. Slowly at first and then, realizing that the unpleasant George Brent was dead, faces began to lighten and voices were cheerfully raised. Someone even shook Bill's hand as though he had done the community a favour. He found himself back in the saloon with somebody buying him a drink and with a noisy throng of men around him.

They dispersed after a while but one man remained. He was a short, fat fellow, nearly bald and with an open face that was tanned and lined by the weather. He ordered another beer for himself and for Bill. They drank silently for a few moments.

'You done this town a favour,' he said quietly, 'but I guess you already know that. I'm Dale Braden. George was my brother-in-law.'

Bill looked at the cheerful face of the man.

'Have I left a grievin' widow?' he asked contritely.

'Hell, no. Dorothy upped and left the bastard years ago and took the kids with her. I guess she owns his business now, and it will be one real pleasure to write and let her know about it. How did the shootin' come about? Or shouldn't I ask?'

Bill decided to tell part of the story. These people were so far from the beaten track that they might not even know of the missing stage.

He told his tale and the man listened passively. He shook his head when it was over and took the fresh beer that

68

Bill had bought him.

'Well, if that don't beat the band,' Dale Braden muttered softly. 'A Wells Fargo stage and the whole caboodle with it. Are you a lawman, fella?'

Bill smiled. It was the third time he had been asked that question since coming to town.

'No, I'm investigatin' for a minin' company that had some gear on board,' he explained.

The man nodded.

'Well, I can't help you much,' he said, 'but you picked the right town. A fella rode in about a week or two ago. He was ridin' a mule and leadin' three others. Took a drink here in the saloon and asked Mike if we had a horse dealer in the place. Mike sent him round to George and the fella sold him three of the mules. Then he came to see me.'

His glass was empty and he paused significantly while Bill ordered more drinks. The man sipped the brew with noisy pleasure.

'I own the livery stable round here,' he went on as he wiped his mouth. 'I sell rigs and harness. He buys a four-wheeled surrey from me, and a set of gear. Then he hitches up the mule and goes over to the grocery store to load up. Seemed to have plenty of cash money. He sure didn't look the hold-up type. More like any workin' fella, he was.'

'Can you describe him?'

'Well, he were just like all of us, I reckon. He'd be about forty and well built. Not runnin' to fat like me. A few days without havin' a razor near his face, I guess. He were dressed like a cowpoke and spoke real pleasant-like. Seemed a decent sorta fella. Never argued a price and I reckon that both me and George did good deals.'

Dale Braden put down his glass and stood thoughtfully for a moment.

'If he was one of the fellas what robbed the stage,' he said slowly, 'I can understand him wantin' to sell the mules. But why in hell didn't he ride into town on his own horse? And why did he buy a fancy rig?'

Bill Pearce did not answer right away. He had also been wondering about that very point.

6

Bill Pearce was thoughtful as he rode back to Cooper's Creek. He reported to the jailhouse where the two marshals listened with interest to his tale. Ted Payne checked a map and put his finger on the name of Fremont as he nodded his understanding of Bill's reasoning.

'So why a rig and not a horse?' the lawman asked as though speaking quietly to himself. 'That don't make sense.'

'And where would he be headin' from Fremont?' the federal marshal asked.

All three men stood looking at the coloured map that lined one wall of the office. It was a new one, issued officially after statehood. It had always been there more for admiration than for practical use. Until now.

'There is another town,' Ted Payne said as he jabbed with his finger at a particular spot. 'Place called Dryburg up on Valencia Creek. Trouble is, it's deserted now. The copper minin' fellas polluted the water supply and folks had to move out. There was one hell of a scrap there about five years back. Folks raided the minin' company and the federal people had to turn out and threaten to call in the army.'

'I remember it,' Marshal Willard said. 'And then the copper ran out and the whole place was left in ruins. What would be the point in goin' there?'

Bill Pearce felt that he had to contribute something.

'Gettin' rid of the bodies would be easy enough,' he said, 'and we know how they got rid of the mules. But how do you hide a stage coach?'

Ted Payne looked from one to the other.

'Well, I can't go gallopin' off to an empty town,' he said cheerfully. 'I got too much on right here. It's even outside the county lines, if I'm any judge.'

'Looks like it's me and you, young fella,' Marshal Willard grinned. He looked hard at the map. 'Seems to be a good three-day journey. We'll need to take a spare mule with provisions and set out early tomorrow. That all right with you?'

Bill nodded his agreement and the three men went off to their suppers and beds.

* * *

It was a hard ride to Dryburg. A wind blew steadily from the west that drove grit into their faces. The trail was also as bad as could be. With nobody visiting the place and no regular traffic in that isolated direction, what had once been a clearly marked route was now overgrown with mesquite and scrub.

It took the two men four days and they both heaved audible sighs of relief when the ruined buildings came into view. It was a sorry-looking place with walls shedding adobe, and planks fallen from porches and stoops. Winds had scoured off all the paintwork while fencing had collapsed amid tall grasses that were overgrowing everything.

There was a saloon that had no windows or door and where the name board lay across the entrance. A barber shop still flew its striped pole but the colours were faded and the door swung back and forth in the breeze. A horse trough contained a green slime that looked almost solid and a smithy leaned dangerously and shivered every time an extra strong gust shook the ruined building. The two men halted at the beginning of the main street and looked at each other.

'Well, I ain't seen a sight like this before,' Marshal Willard said in as cheerful a voice as he could muster. 'Let's find a place that has a roof and some doors. We'll settle in there, keep the animals close by, and have ourselves a meal. It'll be too dark by then to search the town tonight, but we'll get some sleep and start in the morning.'

Bill nodded and they urged their mounts and the laden mule down the street to stop outside the jailhouse. It still had a door that was closed. The windows had long since broken but there were shutters. The roof seemed sound enough and they steered the animals to the rail and dismounted. The door was not locked and the office lightened up when they drew back the shutters to look around.

There was no furniture, just an old Imperial stove and a single oil lamp hanging from the ceiling. Bill pulled it down and shook the thing gently. There was still fuel in the copper pan. He grinned and lit it. This done, Marshal Willard closed the shutters again to keep out the dust. The room looked more cheerful and they soon had a fire going in the old stove.

The animals were unsaddled and taken round to one of the more secure corrals. Then the two men had a meal, seated on the floor with moths flying around in the warmth of the lamp. They had their blankets and saddles to rest on and were soon asleep.

A couple of hours had passed when Bill felt a sharp dig in his ribs and a hand covering his mouth none too gently.

'Keep quiet, fella,' Marshal Willard whispered urgently. 'There's someone prowlin' around outside. They disturbed the horses just now. Listen.'

Bill sat up and could hear the restless movement of the animals. The room was dark but the stove still gave off a little glow that flickered redly against the wooden walls. The two men pulled on their boots and strapped pistols to their waists. The marshal picked up a shotgun and led the way to the back door of the little place. He opened it gently and the cold night air hit him in the face like a blow as the keen wind almost blew the door from his grasp.

The moon was low in the sky and it

was possible to see that the animals were the only moving things at the back of the jailhouse. They still stirred restlessly as the two men slipped along the side of the building to reach the main street. A figure was hurrying across the rutted ground and Marshal Willard raised the shotgun.

'Stay right there, fella!' he yelled. 'I ain't gonna miss at this range.'

The figure hesitated for a moment and then came to a halt. The two men approached to find themselves facing an elderly man who appeared to be unarmed. He looked to be in his sixties and had a scruffy white beard and seamed red face. His lips were prominent as he opened his mouth to show just a few discoloured teeth.

'I ain't done nothin' wrong,' he pleaded in a whining voice. 'Just wanted to see who was in town. I ain't used to strangers.'

'Let's get outa this wind,' Marshal Willard said in a friendlier voice. 'We'll have a cup of coffee and you can tell us a few things about Dryburg township.'

He led the way back to the jailhouse and Bill lit the oil lamp and a couple of candles. The place looked more hospitable and the coffee was soon heated up. The old man took the tin cup gratefully and looked hard at the two strangers.

'You ain't the fellas who was here last time,' he said. 'I guess you're just passin' through and takin' a bit of shelter from this wind?'

It was a question and he looked hopefully from one man to the other. The lawman displayed his badge and nodded in the direction of his companion.

'I'm a federal marshal and this lad's my deputy,' he said with a sly wink at Bill. 'Have you heard tell of the stage that vanished on the way to Cooper's Creek?'

The old man's eyes glowed with excitement in the light of the candles. He shook his head and listened avidly as they told the story.

'Well, if that don't beat all,' he said when it was over. 'Is there a reward?'

'I reckon so. Tell me about the fellas who was here last time. They sound mighty interesting.'

The old man scratched his face and took another drink of the hot coffee.

'Well, I lives in a shack behind the old saloon,' he said slowly. 'Been there since the time gold was found up the creek. And still lookin' for it and hopin' the day will come.'

He cackled good-naturedly.

'I ain't struck rich so far but a fella's gotta live in hope. The creek pans a few dollars now and then and that just about keeps me goin' for a bit longer. Folks never come near this place. Most of the water's poisoned, and without water, Dryburg won't never open up again. It weren't us goldhuntin' fellas as did it. It was the copper-minin' company. They used steam shovels and tore the land apart. And when they'd made their money, they just moved on.'

He shook his head and stared at the

warm stove for a few moments.

'Then these two fellas came to town,' he said quietly. 'Ridin' mules, they was. Damnedest thing I ever did see. Told me they had some fellas to meet in town and that I should go off and take a few drinks at the nearest waterin' hole. Gave me twenty dollars, they did. I ain't never had twenty dollars all at one time in my life. Believe me, fellas, I was on my mule and headin' for the bright lights before they changed their minds. And they weren't folks to argue with. Big men. Decent-lookin' but big.'

Bill poured them all some more coffee and the old man went on with his story.

'I stayed away for six days, just as they asked. Had a few drinks and bought in supplies while I had the chance. They was gone when I got back here. Nary a trace of them. But they had left somethin' behind.'

He paused as though for dramatic effect and looked archly from one man to the other.

'They left a Concord stage,' he said triumphantly.

Bill Pearce almost spilled his coffee and the marshal's face broke into a wide grin.

'Well, if that don't take the head off the turkey,' he murmured. 'So where is this stage coach now?'

'In the old smithy. They musta wheeled it in and closed the doors. I never go lookin' round the town no more. There ain't anythin' left worth havin' these days. But the smithy door had been repaired, and I sure as hell noticed that. When I opened up, there was this rig. Plain as plain.'

'We gotta see this,' Bill said eagerly. He started for the door but Marshal Willard raised a restraining hand.

'We can't do anythin' useful till daylight,' he said, 'and the thing ain't goin' no place fast.'

He turned to the old man.

'Was there anythin' on board the stage?'

The gold miner shook his head sadly.

'Coupla water bottles,' he said, 'and a kit of tools to fix the wheels and stuff like that. Weren't no money, if that's what you was hopin' for.'

Marshal Willard grinned. 'It was, but we didn't expect them to leave it for us. What's your name?'

'Seth. Folks just call me Old Seth and I reckon that'll do for the time I've got left. Is there any reward for findin' the stage?'

His voice was eager and the lawman felt reluctant to disappoint the old fellow.

'I figure there'll be a few dollars comin' to you, Seth,' he said reassuringly. 'Anythin' else you can tell us?'

'I reckon not.' The old man's voice was loaded with regret.

Seth left soon after and the two went back to their disturbed sleep after another drop of coffee improved by a touch of the marshal's whiskey. Bill dropped off with surprising ease and woke as the birds were making a noise above the jailhouse porch. Marshal

Willard was already up and cooking bacon on the stove. They ate quickly and then went out to find the smithy and take a look at what had been discovered there.

Seth was already on the scene, anxious to keep in touch with the people who would be giving him a few dollars. He had flung back the wind-scoured doors of the derelict building to disclose the only thing it housed.

Marshal Willard let out an almost audible sigh of satisfaction at finding the rig he had been seeking for so long. He walked all round it, slowly touching the worn woodwork with his hands. Then he opened one of the doors and looked inside. He examined the seats and peered around the shabby interior.

'Well, there's no blood,' he said as he came round to the driver's box. 'No sign of violence at all. Not a bullet hole or any other damage that I can see.'

He climbed up and checked the long seat. He looked disappointed as he scrambled down again to inspect the mass of mule harness on the ground.

'It just don't make sense,' he muttered before turning his attention once more to old Seth.

'When these fellas sent you outa town,' he said thoughtfully, 'where did you go? Fremont'

'Hell, no. That's too far away. I went to a little place less than a day's ride from here. It's just a collection of Mexican adobe huts built near a creek. Got a store and a drinkin' place, but ain't got nothin' much else to boast about.'

Marshal Willard scratched the side of his face and looked to Bill for inspiration. The young man had no useful opinion. He felt as baffled as the federal officer.

'Looks like we're back where we started,' the lawman said mournfully. 'We'd better do the best we can anyways. We'll strip out the seats, check again for bullet holes, and see if any of this harness is damaged. I don't figure on leavin' here until I have every last bit of information on this damned rig.'

'I'll leave you fellas to it then,' Seth said. 'I'll put some coffee on to boil and you can join me when you've finished here. My place is the shack just behind the saloon. You can't miss it 'cos it's the only place in town with smoke comin' outa the stove pipe.'

He cackled at his own wit and went off down the street. Bill and the marshal began to search the rig with more care and were soon sweating as the heat of the day descended on the empty town. It was nearly an hour before Marshal Willard threw down the last piece of harness in disgust and stood watching Bill check the bottom of the rear baggage rack. They shook their heads at each other to show that nothing had been found that was of any value in their search.

One newspaper from Tombstone, a small pocket knife, and a couple of coins were all there was to show for their efforts.

Bill climbed down from the rig while

the lawman brushed his own pants with a grubby hand. They were both ready to leave when a sudden shadow drew their attention to the doorway.

A man stood darkly against the strong sun. He was tall and thin, dressed rather like some sedate preacher in black frock coat and white stock. But he held a cocked pistol in each hand.

7

'Where are the women?'

The voice was harsh and cut like a jagged blade. Bill Pearce and the marshal looked at the steadily held guns and at the sour face of the man who stood before them. His mouth was a thin, straight line with long ridges at each side. His eyes were deeply sunk and of a colour that could not be judged in the poor light. He moved forward and surveyed the two men coldly.

'I asked a question,' he said as he made a slight gesture with the Colt in his right fist.

'We'd like to know that,' Marshal Willard answered with a slow move of his hand to pull back the coat and show his badge. 'I'm a federal marshal and this here fella is workin' for a minin' company that had some freight on this stage. So who the hell are you?'

The stranger looked hard at the two men and then glanced at the rig.

'Nothin' there?' he asked anxiously.

'Not a spot of blood or a bullet hole. Now, suppose you put those guns away and we hear your story.'

The man looked uncertain for a moment but gave a sudden start as he felt the barrel of a weapon prodding his back. It was Seth. The old man had come quietly through the open doorway and pressed a shotgun firmly against the stranger's body.

'Drop them guns, fella,' the old man ordered with surprising authority. 'I ain't fussy about shootin' folk that dresses like lawyers.'

The man dropped the weapons to the ground and stood helplessly while Bill picked them up. Seth prodded his victim further into the smithy and gave a wide grin as he let the marshal take control of events.

'I reckon I sure earned a bigger slice of that reward,' the old man chuckled.

'Ain't had so much fun since the Abilene whorehouse burned down.'

'Now suppose you start talkin' to us all friendly-like,' the marshal suggested to the stranger. 'I don't like folk pointin' guns at me. And I'm real interested in fellas involved in this stage business. So who the hell are you?'

The man tried to smile but it was not something he seemed accustomed to doing.

'I'm Cy Owens,' he said slowly, 'and I'm what you might call a hired hand to find out what happened to the two women on this stage.'

'And who hired you?'

The man shook his head.

'I can't name names,' he said, 'but the fella's wife was travellin' on the stage from Tombstone to Cooper's Creek. She was wearin' some valuable jewellery and was surely worth robbing. I'm bein' paid to find out what happened to her.'

'So that would be Mrs Smith,' the marshal said quietly. 'Why was she goin' to Cooper's Creek? It ain't exactly the place for a wealthy woman to do her shopping.'

'Mrs Smith had business there.'

'Is that a fact now? I seem to be surrounded by fellas workin' away like Pinkerton agents. So who the hell is Mrs Smith?'

'I can't tell you that. And the name is not the real one.'

'Funnily enough, I sorta guessed that. Well, here we are with an empty stage, four missin' people, and a coupla fellas who don't seem to be helpin' me much. The young fella here has at least done the best he can, and between us, we've gotten ourselves this far and located the stage. I take it you've been tailin' us?'

The man nodded. 'You two were the only leads I had,' he admitted.

'Yeah, well, have you got anythin' useful to throw into the pot? After all, you are an investigator of sorts, and us fellas gotta stick together.'

'I've not found out anythin' much,'

Cy Owens shrugged. 'I checked at Silverton and found you'd already been there. Then I tried Cooper's Creek and heard that you'd just left town. I set off after you and landed in this place.'

There was a short silence while the lawman considered the position. It was Seth who broke the awkward pause by announcing that he had coffee on the boil at his shack. Cy Owen was given back his guns and they left the smithy and crossed the street to the little cabin. The home of Dryburg's only resident was tucked away down a short lane behind the saloon.

It was a surprisingly neat place with a sound roof and some good pieces of furniture. An old dog slept in front of the stove and only opened one bleary eye to look at the newcomers. The room was warm and the coffee was bubbling away.

'You're sure as hell comfortable here, Seth,' the marshal said as he seated himself on a clean bentwood chair.

'I works rough, Marshal, but I likes

my comfort,' the old man chuckled. 'When all the folks left Dryburg, I went around and helped myself to what bits of furniture they'd not wanted. Then I mended the roof of this place, moved in the stove from the dry goods store, and set up real snug.'

He placed enamel mugs in front of his guests and the marshal lifted the strong brew to sniff it appreciatively. Then something occured to him.

'Folk left this town because the water supply was bad,' he said suspiciously. 'Where does your drinkin' water come from, Seth?'

The old man grinned. 'You ain't gonna be poisoned,' he told him. 'There's a well back of here. It ain't much but I can get pure drinkin' water from it. All filtered through the sand, it is, and clean as a preacher's mind.'

'That don't really cheer me up,' the marshal said sourly. 'I've known too many preachers.'

He took a sip of the coffee and nodded his approval. The four men chatted for a while and Cy Owens became a little more friendly. He explained that like Bill, he was a freelance agent who struggled to make a living in cases like the present one. They discussed the next move while Seth got down the big round tin of Sunnyside coffee and added to the brew. He produced his latest find of gold scraps. It was just a mixture of dust and tiny granules that were housed in a chamois bag and must have weighed all of half an ounce. That was a triumph in Seth's rheumy old eyes. He could live on the seven or eight dollars' value for a couple of weeks or more.

'So what happens next?' Cy Owens asked after a while.

The marshal pushed away his empty mug and sat back in the chair.

'Well, we could be at a dead end,' he said thoughtfully. 'There's nothin' here that helps, so I think that Bill and me will be headin' back for Cooper's Creek. There's at least a telegraph there and we can keep in touch with the rest of the world. What do you aim to do?'

The man shrugged. His sour face seemed to be more lined as the little cabin grew darker with the changing direction of the sun.

'I'll just go on huntin' around at every town I can reach,' he said. 'Somebody must know somethin' worth while.'

The marshal leaned forward.

'But don't tail us again,' he advised quietly. 'I had you picked out as far back as our first halt. You did a good job, fella, but I'm an old hand at this sorta thing, and I don't like folk followin' me around.'

Cy Owens dropped his eyes for a moment and then looked up again to glare at the lawman.

'I'll go where the hell I wanta go,' he said, 'and no federal man will get in my way. You had the drop on me back there with the help of this old fool. But I don't aim it should happen again.'

'Then go your ways, fella, and try

tradin' under your own name next time you meet me.'

There was a silence that was only broken by Seth knocking two of the enamel mugs together as he stowed them angrily on the shelf again.

'You think you're one smart hombre, Marshal,' Cy Owens said as he stood up and towered over the federal man. 'So what do you reckon my name is then?'

'I heard tell of a fella called Brad Webster who runs a cattle-dealin' business outside Tombstone. Just about fits your description. Right down to the guns and the black, go-to-meetin' suit. I figure as how you ain't no hired hand but the boss man himself. And tryin' to find a missin' wife and a lotta cash money she was carryin' with her. Am I wrong?'

Cy Owens' mean face glared in fury and his hand went down for the gun at his right hip. He drew and pulled back the hammer with frantic speed. Two weapons exploded at almost the same time.

The acrid smoke was choking in the little cabin and hung in layers on the air. Marshal Willard still sat in the chair, a gun just showing above the table top as he looked at Cy Owens with a slight smile on his broad face. The thin man had reeled back against the wall. He still held his own Colt but blood trickled from a gash along his right forearm and he stared at the steadily held pistol in front of him.

He mouthed an unspoken curse as he holstered his own gun and rushed from the cabin. Seth made to follow but Marshal Willard raised a restraining hand.

'Let him go,' he ordered. 'He might be of more use to us alive.'

The old man put down the shotgun that he had grabbed and turned back with bad grace.

'I coulda finished the bastard,' he complained. 'He called me an old fool, he did.'

'He took us all for fools,' the lawman said as he crossed to the little window and looked out. The back lane was empty and Cy Owens or Brad Webster had vanished.

'I reckon he's headin' outa town to find a doctor,' Bill suggested. 'That was surely one good shot, Marshal.'

'I was expectin' trouble and I didn't want him followin' us around any more.'

'Is he really the fella from Tombstone?' Bill asked.

'Yeah, he fills the bill. I sorta knew the face but just couldn't place it. And then it came to me and I took a stab at seein' how he'd act if I mentioned Brad Webster's name. He sure took the bait.'

'We need somethin' stronger than coffee,' old Seth suggested.

He crossed to a small wood plank-chest and brought out a jar of corn mash.

'Ain't fancy stuff but it hits the spot,' he said as he took down the mugs again.

Bill watched as the old man poured out the yellowish brew. He leaned towards the lawman with a raised eyebrow.

'You're lookin' very pleased with yourself, Marshal,' he suggested.

Willard grinned. 'I am, son. I'm just about beginning to see what this could all be about. We've got to get to Cooper's Creek and send off a telegraph message to Tombstone. Marshal Earp can help out if my ideas are right. You might get back that freight parcel yet, my lad.'

8

His right arm was aching. The tight bandage that he had made from his bandanna seemed to make matters worse. He rode through the gathering dusk towards the only town he knew where a doctor would be available. He spurred his horse angrily to reach Cooper's Creek as soon as possible.

Marshal Willard had been right. The rider's name was really Brad Webster. He was a cattle dealer from a few miles outside Tombstone and was well known among certain folks for buying animals that needed their brands changing or moving to another part of the country before they were put on sale again. Brad Webster had made a lot of money and had plenty of enemies. His wife was the biggest one.

And now she had left him. He had come home after a short buying trip to find the safe open and all his ready cash missing. Over seven thousand dollars and a collection of gold coins. Brad Webster was not a man to stand humiliation and he was determined to avenge himself on the woman.

Her rig and one horse were missing and he was able to trace them to Tombstone where a Mrs Smith had taken the stage to Cooper's Creek. But it never reached Cooper's Creek and the last he knew of it was the stop for a change of mules at Silverton.

He had pursued every line he could find and had ended up by having to follow the federal marshal and some young fellow as they crossed the countryside in their own search. And now he had one useless arm and was none the wiser than before. He allowed himself a sour grimace as he rode. He could at least use a gun with the other hand. Brad Webster did not know the word for it, but he was really ambidextrous, which was the reason he always carried two Colt.44s.

He had to rest up eventually but slept badly before rushing on in the early light. His arm had numbed and he and his horse were exhausted when Cooper's Creek was finally reached. It was past ten in the evening and the lights of the town were a welcome sight as he rode down the main street and past the busy saloon. He drew rein outside the doctor's house behind the hardware store.

There were lights on and Brad Webster drew a sigh of relief as he dismounted and tethered the animal to a fence. Doctor Rogers himself opened the door and ushered the man into the warm and neatly furnished building. He took in the situation at once and led the way to the surgery where he was soon at work on the long gash the bullet had caused.

'So what you been doin' to yourself?' he asked cheerfully as he cleaned the wound.

'I was out buyin' cattle along Elmsmore way and took a fall from my horse. Caught my arm on some fencing,' Brad Webster explained.

He knew that the injury did not look like a bullet wound and thought it easier to lie. The large medical man with the round, cheerful face did not seem perturbed by the answer and merely went on with his work.

'I was here in town a few days ago,' Brad went on. 'There seemed to be some trouble over a stage that's gone missin' on the way from Tombstone. What was it all about?'

Doc Rogers told him and mentioned the near-lynching of one of the hold-up men. Brad Webster's eyes became alert.

'And you still got this fella in the jailhouse?' he asked as casually as he could manage.

'Yep, until the county sheriff comes to collect him. It's one of the oddest things I ever did come across. How in hell do you lose a Concord stage and all the folks aboard?'

'Sounds real strange,' Bert agreed as he winced at the medico's attentions.

'And this hold-up fella, didn't he know anythin' useful?'

'No, and Marshal Payne ain't the talkative type. But I hear tell that somebody here in town has been tippin' off these hold-up fellas. Name of Alex Cullen, so folks tell me. But there ain't nobody of that name in Cooper's Creek.'

'Is that a fact now? It sure is one hell of a puzzle.'

Brad Webster left the surgery a short time later. His arm was well bandaged and the doctor had been fair in his charges. He had even given the patient a couple of powders to take if the pain became too much to bear. Brad Webster rode down the main street and looked at the windows of the jailhouse. The place was in darkness and locked up. He rode round to the back and found that the heavy door there was also fastened.

He left his mount behind the jailhouse and walked across the main street to the Golden Horse saloon.

There were still quite a few customers and most of them were the late drinkers who had swallowed a few too many. The deputy marshal was easy to pick out. He was a young fellow, well built, and with a flushed face. He had beer and a whiskey glass in front of him and Brad Webster went to the bar to quietly order a beer for himself.

He waited patiently until the groups of noisy regulars began to split up and head for their beds. There was no sign of the marshal as the deputy left the saloon and slowly weaved his way up the main street. He reached a small lane that was narrow and unlit and turned into it.

Brad bent down to remove his spurs. He then looked round to make sure that nobody was about. He followed the young man down the lane and drew his gun as he neared him. He struck the blow with savage force and his victim collapsed with only a slightly surprised gasp as he tumbled against a wooden wall. Brad Webster took no chance. He struck again to make sure and then searched the pockets of the fallen man. The keys were there and he hurriedly went back to the main street where he strolled quite slowly towards the jailhouse.

He headed down the side lane to the rear door. There was not enough light to see by and he had to try three keys from the ring before one of them fitted. The door swung open and a musty smell wafted out. He felt his way down a short corridor with a room on either side. Then another door admitted him to the main office of the building with two cells set in the left-hand wall. The shutters kept the room dark and he risked striking a vesta and holding it in his cupped hand.

One of the cells was occupied. A man lay on the bunk and woke with a start as the sudden noise of the striking vesta disturbed him. He sat up and peered through the bars.

'You ain't the lawman,' Bert Blansky said as he screwed up his eyes to see who was behind the light.

'No, I ain't,' Brad Webster said quietly. 'I figure as how the marshal is in his bed right now, and I can tell you for sure that the deputy fella ain't movin' from where I left him. You want outa here?'

'I sure do.' Bert jumped up and came over to the bars. 'The keys are in the top drawer of the desk. Right where you are now. Who are you, fella?'

'I could be the man who saves you from a long term in the county jail. If you tell me what I want to know.'

Brad Webster opened the desk drawer and felt about for the cell keys. He took them out and rattled them in front of the prisoner. The vesta, held in his other hand, went out and they were in darkness again.

'What do you want to know?' Bert's voice held an edge of desperation.

'Well now, I want you should tell me all about this stage you was supposed to be robbing,' Brad Webster said as he seated himself on the edge of the desk.

'Tell me everythin' that happened.'

Bert told the story, and included the killing of their partner and the later death of his own brother as he tried to rob the gun store. The thin man listened patiently, hardly moving in the cool darkness.

'So you never got to meet this Cullen fella?' he asked.

'No, only Al knew who it was, and let slip that Cooper's Creek was the place. That's why we came here, so that we could team up.'

Brad Webster rose to his feet and threw the keys angrily on the desk. He headed for the door.

'You ain't no use to me then,' he said brutally. 'This Cullen fella could be my only lead, and you ain't headin' me in his direction.'

'Wait!'

Bert's voice was suddenly loud and almost hysterical in the confined space.

'I can help you, but you gotta get me outa here. They aim to try me for Al's killin' as well as plannin' to rob the stage. I could hang, fella. You gotta get me outa this place.'

Brad Webster turned and came back to the bars. There was a slight grin on his face that the darkness hid.

'Lookit,' he said quietly, 'you help me and I'll help you. I ain't playin' games here so just tell me what I want to know.'

Bert nodded anxiously. 'Well, just after the locals had tried to lynch me, this old preacher fella comes into the jailhouse. He told the marshal about me and Hank askin' about Alex Cullen, and then he told them who Alex Cullen was.'

'Did he now? And who the hell is he?'

Bert told him and the cattle dealer gave a long, low whistle. He picked up the keys again and opened the cell. Bert dashed out as though another lynching party was in pursuit. He nodded his thanks as he stumbled down the rear hallway in the darkness and out into the night air. Brad Webster followed at his leisure and strolled back to the main street.

He stood looking at the Golden Horse saloon with a slight grin around his thin mouth. The place was near empty now and the staff were clearing up. He watched as the oil lamps were hoisted down and put out. There were lights on in the living quarters above but he still waited until the bar staff came out of the front door, waving noisy farewells to Fred Siddons.

The owner was short and stocky and getting on in years. He carried a gun at his hip but looked a little too old to use it. Brad Webster allowed himself a slight smile. He listened as the door was bolted and the last shred of candlelight vanished from the lower floor of the saloon.

Then he crossed the street. He went down the lane at the side of the Golden Horse and walked quietly along the stoop until he came to a rear door under a porch. The windows on either side of it were shuttered and he turned the brass knob tentatively. To his surprise, the door swung open on silent hinges.

The sudden light took Brad Webster by surprise. He found himself in a small hallway with rooms on either side and a staircase built against one outer wall. There were at least six or seven men and women there, and they all turned to face him.

He had already drawn his gun with the left hand and was now at a loss to know what to do next. He realized vaguely why he had heard nothing from the stoop. Walls and windows were heavily curtained and there were thick coconut mattings under his feet. The women wore make-up and some looked as if they had forgotten to put on all their clothes. That was the moment he knew that the rear door of the Golden Horse was the entrance to the rooms above where the girls plied their trade.

Before Brad Webster could recover his poise, Fred Siddons pushed his way forward. He saw the gun but did not seem impressed.

'Put that thing away, fella.' he bawled. 'We don't like rough stuff around here. So either behave yourself or get the hell out.'

'I want Alex Cullen,' the cattle dealer snarled.

There was a silence in the place and Fred Siddons turned slightly pale under the warm glow of the lamps.

'Ain't never heard of him,' he shouted dismissively. 'Just go your way, fella.'

His hand went down for the gun at his belt and he drew it with a speed that nobody would have expected from an ageing man of his bulk. It was not fast enough. Brad Webster fired and the saloon owner looked at his opponent in surprise. Then he seemed to realize that he had been hit. He tried to say something but staggered as two of the screaming women ran to his aid. A man on the stairs pulled a gun and took a wild shot at Webster. He missed and the cattle dealer fired back as he dashed out of the place. He blundered past one of the girls who tried to stop him, and took a final, parting shot in case anyone was pursuing him.

Nobody did and Brad Webster was able to reach his horse and leave town before the law turned up.

It was Marshal Payne who was summoned from his bed by somebody who heard the shooting and had seen something of the commotion at the back of the saloon. The lawman arrived with a shotgun under his arm. He was followed at a discreet distance by some of the town worthies. The mayor was behind the doctor, but nobody outpaced the mortician who arrived in shirt-sleeves and still wearing his reading glasses.

Fred Siddons lay against the stairs, clutching his stomach and his face pale and without expression. His weeping wife knelt at his side and the girls fussed around without being of any real use. Doc Rogers took over but shook his head sadly when he saw the wound.

The marshal listened to the story that everybody tried to tell at the same time. He pulled a face at the mention of Alex Cullen.

'If that fella was after Alex Cullen,' he said grimly, 'he sure got the wrong one.'

9

Bill Pearce and the federal marshal rode back to Cooper's Creek at a leisurely pace. Bill was anxious to know what the lawman could tell him about Brad Webster. He did not have long to wait.

'I heard tell of Webster quite a few years back,' Marshal Willard said quietly as they rode. 'The local lawmen were all certain sure that he was buyin' stolen cattle. They could never quite prove it because the animals were sold far enough away to make it difficult to check. Some of them went across the border. If the brand was an easy one to change, then they ended up in local sales. He's one smart and crooked operator. And one real nasty son of a bitch.'

He took off his hat to fan himself in the heat of the day. The sun was high and there was no breeze.

'We gotta stop soon,' he said. 'These horses need a drink almost as much as I do. We'll try that trickle of water that folks with bad eyesight call Fulsome Creek. Now, where was I? Ah, yeah. Webster married a real feisty woman who helped him make his money, and could take care of herself if anybody pulled a gun. Good-looker she was too. Then I hear tell that things went sour. He beat up on her and she left him a coupla times. But they seemed to get together again after a few months. I'm wonderin' if she's gone again. But taken a load of cash money with her this time. That's the only reason he'd be out lookin' for her.'

The lawman chuckled at the thought.

'I'll send a telegraph message to Virgil Earp and ask him what's happenin' up his way. He'll have heard if the Websters are missin' from their usual haunts. Then we'll know we're right about it. And that'll lead us to the next stage of the hunt. If you still want to ride alongside of me.'

He looked at his companion.

'I sure do. We make a decent team, Marshal,' Bill said with a grin.

'Fair enough, lad, and my name's Phil. Y'see, I happen to know that Ma Webster has a brother down Simancas way. He's got a small cattle spread there and folks tell me that he won't have no dealings with Brad Webster. If I were his sister and I was gettin' away from an unwanted husband with a bag full of his money, I'd be inclined to go join my kin. Sound logical?'

Bill nodded. 'Sure does. But won't Webster think of that?'

'Sure, if he imagines that she's still alive. But her brother has his ranch hands and Webster is alone. He also has a damaged right arm. The odds won't be even if they do meet up.'

'So what do you think happened to that stage, Phil?' Bill asked the question tentatively. Using the marshal's given name did not feel quite right and he hesitated at the familiarity of it. He had never spoken to a federal marshal like that before.

'Well, that's the real question,' the lawman sighed. 'I figure as how somebody held it up before it reached the spot where them three fellas was waiting. It's just possible that Alex Cullen gave that information to two parties. Just to be on the safe side. That's somethin' we must take up with Marshal Payne when we reach Cooper's Creek. Alex Cullen has got to be put in the jailhouse and questioned. Nobody seems to have been injured on the stage and it's possible that the raiders took everybody to Dryburg. One of them rode in, knowin' that old Seth was somewheres around, and paid him to leave the place for a few days. Then they brought the stage in, took off everythin' worth having and then went on to Fremont to sell the mules. It sounds like it was all well planned.'

'And what about the driver, guard, and the two women?' Bill asked doubtfully. 'What would they do with them?'

'That's what worries me, son. They

might have killed them back at Dryburg and their bodies could have been dumped in one of the old minin' tunnels. We'd never have a hope of findin' them. And there's another thing that troubles me. I just can't make sense of it at all. Why ride a mule into Fremont and into Dryburg? Seth was right about that, y'know. If they held up the stage, they must have had their own horses. So why use one of the mules?'

'If Ma Webster never reached her brother's place, how can he help us?'

'He could have known she was plannin' to run off,' the marshal replied thoughtfully. 'I'm bankin' on her havin' sent him a letter tellin' him to expect her. In fact, I wouldn't mind bettin' that he was waitin' to meet her at Cooper's Creek. That could be why she booked to that place. He probably headed for home when the stage didn't show up, and he could be doin' a bit of searchin' himself right now. It's one hell of a mystery.'

Bill nodded. 'Maybe the marshal of

Cooper's Creek will have some news for us when we get there,' he suggested. 'We certainly have some for him. Do you think he'll have dealt with Alex Cullen?'

★ ★ ★

Marshal Payne had not dealt with Alex Cullen. He had been too busy getting a posse together. Fred Siddons was popular and men were eager to join it. They had hurriedly saddled up and a group of twenty or more was soon heading out of town to try and pick up the trail of Brad Webster. Somebody reported seeing him heading north at a furious pace and there was a real determination to get the killer. Nobody bothered much about young Bert Blansky. He was just a common bandit and news of him would be spread through the wanted lists that would soon flood all the local communities.

While Marshal Willard and Bill Pearce still made their way to Cooper's

Creek, the town was getting ready for two funerals. The deputy marshal did not recover from the blows rained on him by Brad Webster. He died in the doctor's surgery without recovering consciousness. The mortician and his assistant worked all night on their preparations while neighbours comforted the saloon keeper's widow. Mrs Siddons presented herself in black, and flanked by the mayor and his wife she walked behind the hearse to the burying plot behind the meeting house.

She was a fine figure of a woman, though well past middle age. She had kept her looks and the flesh on her tear-stained face was firm and unwrinkled.

The little preacher scurried around in his usually aimless fashion, but when it came to speaking, his voice was loud and firm. He could be heard by all as he went through the ritual he had used a thousand times. The more important mourners returned to the saloon where a meal was laid out for them. They stood around enjoying the free drinks and chatting about events in their usually quiet town.

The mayor looked at his watch with a slight frown and whispered in his wife's ear. He had the deputy's funeral to attend in the early afternoon, and had a little job to complete before that event.

He went quietly upstairs to the living quarters where Ma Siddons had retired after greeting the guests. She sat in a darkened room and welcomed the mayor with thanks for his support in her hour of need. He sat down opposite her and went through the ritual of murmured condolences while she listened patiently and wiped her eyes.

'Have you any plans for this place?' he asked quietly. 'The Golden Horse is quite a responsibility for a widow woman without kin.'

'I'll keep it on,' she said bravely. 'Fred would wish that. I always ran the girls' side of things and he managed the rest. Will Thorne can take over downstairs. He's a good bartender and been with us a lot of years. I'm sure I can trust him.'

The mayor shook his head sadly. 'I feel that it could all be a little too much for you,' he murmured. 'Let me put it this way. Folks talk, and if they were to find out that you had been passin' on what your drunken customers told the girls, they wouldn't be well pleased. Everybody calls you Betty, but a few of us remember you as Alexandra Cullen before you married Fred. And that federal marshal is sure to come back to town.'

The woman's face had stiffened as she stared at the stout man who's sweaty face glowed with the heat of the room.

'You remember one hell of a lot, Aaron Stromer,' she said in a new, harsh voice.

'I do. The preacher got scared and went tellin' tales at the jailhouse. When the lawmen have sorted out a few other things, they'll be arrestin' you. I can't stop them, and you'll as sure as hell go to the county jail. I'm just about the only fella who can be of help right now. We've been friends for years and I don't aim to let my friends down.'

Ma Siddons tucked the handkerchief into her sleeve and faced the mayor boldly.

'And what do you get out of it, Aaron?' she asked.

The First Citizen smiled.

'You judge me well, Betty,' he conceded. 'I've always wanted to own this place, and as you say, Will Thorne could run it for me. Just as he would for you.'

'And what about the girls?'

'They might have to move out,' Aaron Stromer said sadly. 'I don't think my lady wife would countenance that sort of thing. She's a real go-to-meetin' sort of body.'

The widow's alert eyes were calculating as she considered the situation.

'Wouldn't you have some explainin' to do yourself?' she asked. 'After all, if Ted Payne comes to arrest me and finds me long gone and you the new owner of this place, that's gonna look mighty strange. Could even mean a new mayor. After they'd lynched the old one.'

Mayor Stomer smiled as he shook his head.

'I ain't been told any of this officially,' he said. 'I'm just a friend of the bereaved, buyin' the saloon so that she can go join her kin in some distant town. If it turns out that she was tippin' off hold-up fellas, then nobody told me about it. And that ain't right, you know. After all, I'm the mayor and I should have been kept informed by the marshal.'

'And how the hell did you find out? Did that damned preacher come croakin' to you as well?'

'No. Mel Ridley was my nephew as well as deputy marshal. It was only right that he should tell his uncle what was goin' on. The lad couldn't get to me fast enough.'

'And now he's dead,' the woman said softly, 'and can't contradict you.'

'That's right, Betty,' Mayor Stromer smiled happily. 'So can we do a deal? You ain't got much time.'

Ma Siddons got to her feet and crossed the room to a small cabinet. She took out a cut-glass decanter and poured them both a shot of whiskey. There was a look on her face that the mayor found a little unnerving.

'Well?' he asked anxiously. 'Have we got a deal? I'll pay a fair price.'

Ma Siddons stood in front of him with the glass twirling in her hands.

'Before you go chasin' off on a stampede, Aaron,' she said silkily, 'just try thinkin' about somethin' real important. As you rightly said, fellas come to see my girls, and they talk. Then the girls chat about it afterwards, and I listen. But who are those fellas, Aaron?'

The mayor opened his mouth to say something, and then began to have a sudden fear that he was losing control of the situation.

'So who are they, Aaron?' she

repeated. 'Let me give you a few hints. There's the fella from Wells Fargo. There's that weasel from the telegraph office. And there's three respectable fellas from the bank. Then we get visits from your deputy. Mel was a great talker. Liked folk to know how important he was. Y'see, Aaron, if anybody tries anythin' with me, I can name a few names. Names you wouldn't want named. Understand me?'

'You're bluffing.' The words were almost strangled.

'Try me. Then again, I wonder how many other businesses in town are payin' a few dollars a week to the mayor so that the council don't make any laws we wouldn't like. When you start talkin' about the county jail, just remember that you could be joinin' me there. So why don't we just work together, like always?'

The mayor looked at his whiskey as if it had suddenly gone sour. There was a confidence about the woman that he had not expected.

'How do you suggest we work together then?' he asked tentatively.

Ma Siddons sat down again and made no attempt to hide the triumph of her smile.

'I don't aim to leave this town,' she said firmly, 'and you sure intend to stay as mayor until you've stolen enough to go live in some big city up north. We got a lot in common, Aaron Stromer. You protect me against them marshals, and I'll tell you somethin' that they'll love to hear. And it'll be the mayor of this town that gives them the information. He'll be the hero.'

'Sounds interesting.'

'You've got to think of all this from some crooked lawyer's point of view. If they did arrest me, they couldn't prove to any court that I'd been arrangin' hold-ups. After all, the fella I told was shot by his partners. And one of his partners is now dead. Then again, I'm a poor female under the control of my husband when all these things happened. A tough fella like my Fred is just the sort to be forcin' me to do these things. A wife has to be obedient. She might get knocked about.'

She smiled sweetly at the mayor and he found it difficult not to smile back.

'I see your point,' he said meekly. 'So I tell the lawmen that they can't make out a case that would stand up in court?'

'That's it, Aaron. But you can tell them that you questioned me, and that it was your cleverness that got the information that you're gonna give them.'

Ma Siddons drank off her whiskey at one gulp and placed the glass firmly on the table at her side.

'Abe Lawson was drivin' that stage, as you already know,' she said slowly. 'He used to visit the girls here in the saloon. He was a quiet sort of fella, and he weren't married. But I was told that he had a woman back in Tombstone. She was already wed to some rich cattle dealer.'

Aaron Stromer's mouth was beginning to open in surprise and delight as he listened.

'Go on,' he urged.

'Will Carr, the guard, was a married man. Never had nothin' to do with my girls. I'd suggested it to him once, and that's how I found out he had a wife. Real faithful husband, he was. Think about it, Aaron. His wife lived in Silverton and one of them passengers boarded there. The other boards in Tombstone. I reckon them marshals will lap up that sort of news. They'll forget all about me.'

Aaron Stromer stood up to go.

'I figure you and me will get on like we always did, Betty,' he said with a grin.

'Not quite, fella,' Ma Siddons said as she stood up herself to show him to the door. 'I don't aim to be payin' you any more money each week. We got too much on each other for that sorta deal, Aaron.'

10

Phil Willard and Bill Pearce reached town the next day. They found the jailhouse locked up and went round to the corral to unhitch their horses and the mule. The mayor came scurrying across the main street to greet them. He opened up the jailhouse and followed them inside. The place smelt fusty and they left the door open to clear the air.

Mayor Stromer told them what had been happening in Cooper's Creek. They heard of the killings and the funerals. Then the First Citizen finally got around to his masterly handling of Ma Siddons. Marshal Willard listened with a slightly cynical expression on his face while Bill lit the stove and put on some water to boil. Both men looked interested when the mayor told his story of the two women who boarded the stage. The marshal glanced at Bill with a slight grin.

'We was on the right lines, lad,' he said cheerfully. 'I guess you did a good job there, Mr Mayor. What you got outa Ma Siddons fits in with what we've been reckonin' on. We've found the stage in an old minin' town out west. Place called Dryburg. There's nothin' left on it, but it all fits in with what we've been workin' at.'

Bill was pleased to be included in the lawman's thoughts and treated as a colleague. He took down the coffee tin and began to brew up a strong-smelling drink. The mayor stressed that the law would never be able to touch Ma Siddons, and that the town needed her in any case. The marshal winked at Bill and they were both extremely cheerful by the time Aaron Stromer left.

'Well, we're sure followin' a live trail, Bill,' Phil Willard said as they drank. 'I reckon that Brad Webster's wife and that stage driver went off with as much money as she could get her hands on. She took the stage at Tombstone and the guard's wife joined them at Silverton. All four of them were in on it. Then they turned off the trail before reachin' here and headed for the empty minin' town.'

Bill nodded as he drank the hot liquid. He felt that the marshal had figured it out well.

'And that would account for the two men ridin' in on the mules that were drawin' the stage,' he murmured. 'They got rid of old Seth for a few days, holed up the rig in the old smithy, and then one of them rode out with the mules to trade for a surrey in Fremont. They needed that rather than horses with women to move about. Then he drove back to Dryburg and the four of them headed out for this fella that's kin to Ma Webster. They sure planned it well.'

'Yeah, and got away with a load of money,' the marshal growled. 'As well as your industrial diamonds. We've still got quite a job catchin' up with them, but at least we have a solid lead. So we go huntin' Ma Webster's brother down Simancas way.'

The marshal swallowed the last of his drink and stood up.

'I'll just go along to the telegraph office and send off a message to Virgil Earp in Tombstone. If he confirms that Ma Webster is missin' from home, we'll know we're right. I dare say Ted Payne has already telegraphed him about her husband. Then we'll lay in more stores and get movin' again. It's a four or five day ride down to Simancas. The spread we want is just west of the town. Her brother's a fella called Ed Wade, and I figure as how we'll find Ma Webster and her stage driver holed up there.'

Phil Willard left the jailhouse and Bill settled down behind the desk with the hot coffee in his cupped hands. He began to feel drowsy and soon put down the cup. It was the marshal's return that woke him from a deep and restful sleep. An hour had passed and the lawman looked pleased with his work.

'Right on the barrel-head, lad,' he crowed. 'Webster rode into Tombstone in one hell of a temper, lookin' for his wife. She'd already left on the stage but the Wells Fargo man knew her by sight even though she used the name of Smith. It's all solved, fella. We just have to catch up with them now.'

* * *

They slept the night at the jailhouse and left town early the next morning. The mule carried plenty of food and water, and the little party moved at a steady pace under the increasing heat of the day. Marshal Payne's posse had still not returned to Cooper's Creek and Phil Willard expressed no great hopes of them catching up with Brad Webster.

It took longer than they had hoped to reach their destination. A week of heat and dust, bad trails and cold nights made the appearance of the little town of Simancas a welcome sight. It was a small place but they were able to stock up with more food there and spend the night in a boarding house while their animals had the comfort of a corral. The locals gave them directions to the Ed Wade spread and they set out again the next morning.

It was not a large ranch but the grazing seemed good and a wide creek flowed through the lower levels of the grassland. There were quite a few cattle about, and some loose horses in the distance. It seemed a decent enough place where a man could live in comfort, well away from prying eyes, and near the Mexican border if a new refuge was needed.

The house was of white adobe with a wide space in front of it and outbuildings on either side. It looked clean and well kept. The rancher was not there and they were greeted by his wife. Ma Wade was a stout woman with a round, healthy face that glistened in the noon-day sun. She took the two men inside when the marshal identified himself as a lawman. A young lad took care of their animals as they were led into a fresh-smelling room.

The hot coffee was welcome and they found themselves sitting in comfortable wicker armchairs that creaked under their weight.

'We don't often get visitors,' Ma Wade said as she offered more coffee. 'What brings you to these parts, Marshal?'

Phil Willard had noticed the anxiety in her voice and the slight trembling of her hands. He knew that he was on the right track.

'Well, it's your husband's sister, Bess Webster,' he said quietly. 'She's up and vanished, and folks is real worried about her. It was suggested that she might have made the journey down here to pay a visit to her kin.'

'No.' The word came out too quickly to be believed. 'We ain't seen hide nor hair of her in a coon's age.'

'Is that a fact? She seems to have walked out on Brad Webster, taken a stage, and then just plumb disappeared.

We thought she'd been killed in a hold-up at first, but we know different now. We've found the stage tucked away in a deserted town. Nary a mark on it, and four folk just vanished. Brad Webster's awful riled. Seems she made off with some of his money.'

Ma Wade almost managed a smile. 'He's a horrible man,' she said heatedly. 'Time she upped and left him. I don't know how she stuck it so long.'

'Well, she's sure done it now.'

The marshal looked around the well-furnished room. He could smell food cooking and noted that the table was laid for a meal.

'When will your husband be home?' he asked.

'He's due any time now. He and a couple of the hands are cleanin' out a creek up near the ridge. He can't tell you any more than I can.'

'Well, we'll wait for him, if you don't mind, ma'am. There are one or two other things we have to discuss.'

A silence fell on the room, and Ma

Wade excused herself to go check on the cooking. Bill and the marshal sat in uncomfortable silence as she pottered around in the kitchen. It was almost a relief when the door opened and a stout man entered, taking off his dusty hat to beat against the door as he crossed the threshold.

Ed Wade was big and tough-looking. His stoutness seemed to contain plenty of muscle and his deeply tanned face was shaven clean and with an alert and determined expression. He looked at the two men without surprise and it was easy to guess that the lad had already told him of their arrival.

'So what does the law have to do with us,' he asked after they had introduced themselves. 'If my sister has left that coyote Webster, it don't seem to be a matter for federal marshals.'

Phil Willard leaned forward in his chair and looked at the two Wades in silence for a moment.

'I think you folks are missin' out on a lot of real busy happenings in the last few weeks,' he said slowly. 'Maybe I oughta lay it all on the line for you.'

He told them about the disappearance of the stage, and the finding of it again in Dryburg. He also mentioned the activities of Brad Webster and the fact that he was now on the run. Ed and his wife looked at each other and the marshal knew that he had two people on the edge of breaking down.

'If your sister is here, Mr Wade,' he said urgently, 'you sure got yourself one almighty trouble. The law ain't the only thing chasin' her. Brad Webster is fightin' mad probably not an hour behind us.'

He was looking at young Bill as he spoke and his companion realized what his part was supposed to be. He nodded agreement and looked as serious as he could. Ma Wade raised a worried hand to the side of her face while her husband's fist automatically felt for the security of the gun at his waist.

'We ain't scared of Webster,' he said

with a show of bravado. 'I got plenty of hands around the place and we can all use guns.' The marshal shook his head.

'Mr Wade,' he said gravely, 'Brad Webster is a killer. He's already finished off a town deputy and another fella back in Cooper's Creek. My guess is that he dodged the posse and hung around to see what Bill and me was doing. If he ain't tailed us here, then I'm gettin' too old to be a good judge of men. He's probably out there right now, watchin' this house and lookin' for signs of his wife.'

There was a strained silence and all they could hear was the bubbling of a pan in the kitchen.

'You'd better tell him, Ed,' Ma Wade suddenly said in a frightened voice. Her husband looked at her and hesitated for a brief moment. Then he made up his mind.

'I guess there ain't no harm in it,' he said as though defeated. 'Bess wrote us some months back to say that she was plannin' to leave Brad Webster. She'd had enough of the brute. There was another man and she wanted to come here and stay with us until they could make a life of their own some place. She didn't say anythin' about him bein' a stage driver, but she did say she'd be takin' Webster for every bent cent she could get. All this about the stage is news to us. But she just ain't arrived, and we're mighty worried, Marshal.'

Phil Willard stood up and looked hard at the Wades.

'Are you tellin' me the truth?' he asked.

'I sure am. We've been worried sick. I rode into Simancas to see if any of the newspapers had arrived there. There was mention of a missin' stage, but I didn't connect it with Bess at first. Then one of my hands came back last week with a copy of the *Tombstone Epitaph*. It mentioned a Mrs Smith gettin' on the stage at Tombstone. That's when I got real worried. We've been talkin' about what we should do.'

His wife nodded her agreement.

'Then I reckon as how we'd better ride to where we last heard of her,' Marshal Willard muttered. 'If we could stay the night and set out first thing tomorrow, we'd be right obliged.'

'You and your deputy are welcome. We got good food and a warm bunkhouse,' Ed Wade said in a relieved voice.

* * *

The two men were on their way again just after daylight. They had been treated well by the Wades and rode east in better weather with the gusty wind behind them instead of rasping against their faces.

'Do you reckon they was tellin' the truth?' Bill asked.

'Part of it. I'll wager they knew about the plan to use the stage and steal all the cash that was aboard. But we can't prove that, so they ain't gonna be mixed up with courts and judges. But that missin' sister is worryin' Ed Wade like hell. He didn't need much of a dig from his wife to tell us.'

'And you sure put a scare into him by sayin' that Brad Webster was around.'

Phil Willard grinned. 'He's got reason to be scared. Brad Webster followed us every spit and holler of the way, lad.'

'I didn't see nothin' of him, Phil. How the hell do you figure he was tailin' us?'

'The horses was restless the first night we pitched camp. That made me a bit wary. Remember how I arranged things the second night? We could have made our beds right in the lee of that mesquite, but I picked an open spot. That meant that somebody could shelter behind the mesquite. And somebody sure did. Recall what happened?'

Bill thought hard for a moment.

'The birds suddenly woke up and started flyin' around,' he said. 'Brad Webster disturbed them.'

'That's right. The only cover he had was that clump of bushes, but he didn't reckon with the birds. He was there watchin' us.'

'So the posse was wastin' time lookin' for him?'

'Posses often do waste their time. A wise fella just hauls up instead of makin' a dash for it. He stays right near to the place he caused trouble and they go tearin' all over the countryside lookin' for him.'

Bill grimaced. 'There's a lot to learn about this job, I reckon,' he said sadly.

'Give it time, lad. I've had over twenty years of it, and I'm still learnin' every day.'

The marshal suddenly reined in his horse and looked back the way they had come. He turned to Bill with a broad grin on his face.

'I reckon we've gone far enough now, young fella,' he said cheerfully. 'Turn yourself and that mule around and we'll go back and see what happens at the ranch house.'

Bill Pearce stared hard at him for a moment and then began to realise what the lawman had in mind. He swung his animal round and the pack mule followed obediently. They started back the way they had come.

'So I'm learnin' some more,' Bill mused with a slight smile.

'That's right, son. If Brad Webster's been trailin' us, as I'm sure he has, he'll now go to the ranch and have a word with the Wades. He'll have made sure we're clear of the place first. Then he'll check to make sure the hands are all away from the homestead. When he knows it's all quiet, he'll pay his wife's family a not very friendly call. And we'll be waitin' for him when he leaves.'

Bill nodded agreement. 'Supposin' he shoots up on the Wades?' he asked.

'That's their problem, lad. They was lyin' to us and they knew what Webster's wife was plannin' to do. They may even be lyin' when they say she hasn't turned up at their place. I don't think they are, but their story might not convince Webster. Any trouble they get into, they brought on themselves. We'll just stand by and collect the reward on Webster.'

'I'd forgotten about that,' Bill said as he recalled the mayor's passionate announcement.

'It don't pay to forget rewards, Bill. They make all our efforts worth while. So let's just set a trap for Webster and hope we hit pay dirt.'

They travelled on towards the ranch and Marshal Willard handed out one more piece of advice for good measure.

'And when we do come up against Webster, shoot to kill, fella,' he advised grimly. 'We don't want to have to haul him around with us for the next six or seven days. We just need the horse and a few personal things to identify him back in Cooper's Creek.'

11

Ed Wade had finished his meal and was sitting in front of the stove inhaling on a small stogie. He was reaching an age when he felt like taking a short doze in the afternoon before going back to the chores that never seem to-end on a ranch. His wife was busy in the kitchen and he was nodding off when the door suddenly opened without ceremony.

The rancher swung round in his chair to see the figure of his brother-in-law silhouetted against the afternoon sun. He got hurriedly to his feet and tried to look reasonably pleased to see the man.

'Well, I sure wasn't expectin' you, Brad,' he said as calmly as he could. 'This seems to be the day for visitors.'

'You've just had two fellas here,' the cattle dealer grated tersely. 'What did you say to them?'

Ed Wade shrugged. 'What could I tell

them? They was tryin' to find out what happened to that stage, and they reckoned that Bess was travellin' on it. They figured that she had survived and might come here. I told them I knew nothin' from nothing. I ain't heard a word of Bess in a 'coon's age.'

'You're lyin' to me, fella. You and Bess planned all this and she's taken me for a hell of a lotta money. And I want it back. So you'd better start tellin' me the truth. I'm real short of patience right now.'

Ed spread his hands in a gesture of conciliation.

'I don't know nothin' about it, Brad,' he pleaded. 'We're out in the wilds here, and the first I heard of anythin' was when these two federal fellas arrived. Why should Bess come here? They tell me that she ran off with the stage driver and that the guard's wife was with them. The federal fella reckons as how they ambushed the Wells Fargo outfit and then left it all hidden away-like. Knowin' I was her brother, they figured she might come here.'

Brad Webster looked round the room. His eyes were restless as though not sure what to do next.

'So where are the federal men off to now?' he asked.

'I don't rightly know, but they found the stage at some place called Dryburg, and I gather they might be headin' back there. It's the last place they know of that might give them a lead. I'm outa this, Brad. It's between you and Bess. She might be my sister but she's gotten her own life to lead. So it's between you, her, and this stage-drivin' fella she took up with.'

Brad Webster looked at his sweating brother-in-law with contempt. He went to the kitchen, nodded a curt greeting to Ed's wife, and then headed up the stairs to check the rest of the house. The two Wades stood as though transfixed until he came back again and stood in front of them.

'Well, it looks like you ain't hidin' them,' he conceded, 'so I'll be on my way. But if Bess shows up here, you'd better get that money off'n her, fella, and return it to me. I'm killin' mad about this, and don't you folks forget it.'

He stormed out of the house and they watched through the window as he mounted his horse, jabbed in the spurs, and rode off furiously.

'I should'a shot him,' Ed Wade growled with an attempt at bravery now that it was safe. 'If I hadn't taken off my gun . . .'

His wife gave him a look of mild pity and went back to finish the chores in the kitchen. Ed stared out of the window for a few minutes and then made up his mind. He ran to the door and called to the young lad who was working in one of the barns.

'Saddle my horse, Harry, and make it fast.'

He went back into the house and strapped on his gunbelt. He took down a shotgun and loaded both barrels. As he was stuffing more cartridges into his pockets, his wife came from the kitchen, wiping her hands on her apron.

'What are you up to, you damned loon?' she bawled. 'You're no match for Brad Webster. And besides, he's gone his way and left us in peace.'

'I was thinkin' of Bess,' Ed said. 'I reckon he's mad enough to kill her, and I can't let that happen. Besides, she could still turn up and we was promised three hundred dollars. I'm gonna tail Brad carefully and shoot the ass off'n him when he settles down for the night.'

'Well, you just make sure he don't shoot the ass off you, Ed Wade. I don't fancy bein' a widow woman for a few years, and I ain't got another bread-earner lined up for saddlin' yet.'

Ed Wade was on his way a few minutes later. He had no intention of doing more than trailing Brad Webster discreetly and waiting until the man was bedded down for the night. Then he would kill him. It might be cowardly, but it would surely solve a few problems.

He had been riding for no more than about twenty minutes when he heard a shot. The rancher reined in his horse and listened. He could see a few birds flying wildly above a group of leaning sycamores over to his right. There was also a slight haze in the air and Brad Webster's horse had certainly been heading in that direction. The hoof marks were clear in the firm, reddish gravel. Ed Wade hesitated. He waited for other shots but there were none. He dismounted to tether his horse to a clump of bushes.

Ed crept forward slowly, hugging the ground and scared of what might happen. Curiosity was the only thing urging him on and he finally came upon the scene of the shooting. A horse stood tethered to a tree and there was no sign of the rider. It was Brad Webster's animal and Ed Wade licked his lips nervously as he lay on his belly amid the scattered grasses and tried to spot some movement.

Then he saw a slight shivering in one

of the bushes as some dust fell from the leaves and floated on the air. Somebody was kneeling amid the foliage and Ed was pretty sure that it was his brother-in-law. The man was not within safe shooting range and did not appear to be aware of his presence. He seemed to be watching something towards the north. Ed could see the barrel of a Winchester carbine poking out from the bushes as Brad Webster peered from his cover.

The rancher crawled backwards away from the scene. He made it to his own horse and unholstered the shotgun. He did not know what the situation was but the lawmen had not long left and it could be that they were now trying to get Brad Webster. That cheered him up as he crawled back again to keep the man in sight.

Nothing had changed and Ed sweated in the heat as he thought of going back to the ranch. He was no hero and would have liked to leave it to the federal men. But suppose they failed. He did not want his brother-in-law to get out of it alive. He raised his head a little and could just see the dark outline of Brad Webster who lay perfectly still in the jumbled bushes.

Ed Wade felt around in the sandy gravel for a stone large enough to use. His sweating hand found one and he took a last careful look at his target before lobbing it through the air. It rattled among the bushes as he intended and raised a curtain of dust as Brad Webster jumped at the sudden movement. He had given away his place of hiding and Ed Wade grinned as he hugged the earth and waited for what would happen next.

Shots rang out and some stray pellets from a shotgun charge scattered among the mesquite not far from Ed's head. He kept low and dared not look at the results of his labours. Brad Webster fired back at the two men who crouched to his right and left.

They were well concealed and one was using a Winchester while the other cradled a scatter gun. Brad Webster was desperate and dripping with sweat. Not many people could scare the cattle dealer, but this pair had him cornered. His horse had also broken loose. The renewed shooting had made it jerk its head and it found itself suddenly free. It did what every sensible horse would do and left the scene.

Bill Pearce and the federal marshal had been taken by surprise. They had been riding back towards the ranch with the intention of watching Brad Webster leave. They then wanted to ambush him in a suitable place and put an end to the killer. The sight of him galloping towards them in a furiously angry mood was unexpected for both sides. It then became a matter of keeping under cover and taking pot-shots. The interference of Ed Wade had made a difference and the two could now see where Webster was pinned down.

They poured in another volley of shots and he replied with his Winchester. The weapon was difficult to handle; his wounded right arm was still stiff and sore. Brad Webster emptied the carbine and put it aside to take out one of his Colts. He fired blindly in the direction of the shots, but the range was too great for a hand gun and he could not be sure of the position of his enemies.

It suddenly occured to him that it was not a bullet that had shaken the bushes and made him give away his position. It had been some other sort of missile, and that could mean a third enemy who was closer than the federal men. He stole a look around but none of the bushes moved and there was no sign of another human being.

He calculated the distance to his horse but the animal had moved out of sight over a slight ridge. He suddenly felt for the first time in his life that he was in a situation he could not control. Brad Webster bit his lip angrily as he worked out the odds of escaping. He decided to crawl backwards towards the point where his mount had been tethered. He would at least be nearer to it. There were also some taller bushes and trees there that would give better cover. He began to edge out of range of the enemy guns.

Marshal Willard saw the slight movement among the mesquite. He raised the Winchester to his shoulder but hesitated in case the thrower of the missile was in range. The lawman was a little puzzled by what had happened. Something had certainly clattered among the undergrowth and made Webster move slightly. But what had it been? And who was responsible?'

He decided to take the risk. His job was to put an end to a killer, and he pulled the trigger. The bullet missed Brad Webster. It went over his head and hit a thick cactus plant that shivered for a moment as it shed some of its trunk. Bill Pearce emptied one barrel of his shotgun in the same direction, but only the cactus suffered as pieces flew off in a shower of green darts.

It was Ed Wade who called the turn.

Brad Webster backed straight towards the place where the rancher waited with his head down and his limbs trembling slightly at the closeness of the shooting. He suddenly saw the soles of his brother-in-law's boots coming towards him through the bushes. Ed Wade grinned and drew his gun. It was his moment and he raised himself a little as he pulled back the hammer.

Brad Webster had good hearing. The sharp click was like a shot to his taut imagination. He swung round, rising almost to his knees to face this new opponent. A Colt was already in his left hand and he levelled it at the startled rancher.

There was one moment when the two men faced each other, both ready to fire. They were only a few feet apart and Brad Webster was the professional gun. But he had made one mistake.

He could now be seen by Marshal Willard and the lawman took a careful aim at the dark shoulders that just showed among the wealth of mesquite.

He pulled the trigger of the Winchester and Brad Webster slumped forward and collapsed on his side. The pistol fell from his grasp and went off as it did so. The bullet ploughed up the earth and Ed Wade let out a little gasp of relief.

The three survivors stood around the body and Ed received thanks for the part he had played. He also received advice to go home to his worried wife and leave the law to manage things. He nodded eager agreement and departed to tell his family and ranch hands of the bravery he had shown in the face of a professional killer. Ed Wade was a very happy man.

'Go find this fella's horse, Bill,' the marshal ordered his companion. 'We need it as identification and because the animal and the saddle will sure as hell be worth a few dollars. With the guns and the reward, this could be a very profitable day's work.'

Bill ran down the slope and up another ridge that was knee-deep in tangled grasses. The cattle-dealer's animal was grazing happily on the other side of the ridge and he had no trouble getting it under control. The horse had already begun to feel lonely in the emptiness of the surroundings. Even a human being was better company than a few jackrabbits.

Marshal Willard searched the body. The man had a good silver watch and chain. He carried a leather wallet of stogies and a silver vesta case. There was also near to thirty dollars in his pockets. They all added up nicely but there was one other thing that was of even more importance.

Brad Webster's wife had written him a letter when she left. It was bitter and mocking, and it told of another man and of the satisfaction she got out of emptying her husband's safe of every dollar. The marshal had all the identification he needed.

All he had to do now was to locate the missing widow.

12

The two men looked down the slope to the dismal view of ruined buildings and a main street over-grown with bushes and tufted grass. Dryburg was as empty and derelict as the last time they saw it. The little mining town even had a smell of decay. A thin wind seemed to whistle in contempt as it passed through the crumbling wooden walls of the rotting structures.

'We gotta start from here,' the marshal said for the umpteenth time. 'Old Seth might remember somethin' that didn't seem important at the time. There'd be wheel marks from the rig that took them outa town. He might have noticed the direction they was heading.'

'If the four of them were in on it,' Bill said slowly as they urged their mounts down the slope, 'then they must have been goin' towards Ed Wade's place.

That won't help us.'

'No, it won't. But look at it from their point of view. Ed is expectin' his sister and her friends. I reckon he's gonna get a share of what they've stole. But suppose they decided to cut him out. Maybe they felt safe enough to go some other place. They had a good rig, all that money, and nobody was likely to find the stage too quickly. They might have changed their plans.'

They rode down the main street, disturbing rodents and birds as they moved. Seth's little shack was a welcome sight with smoke coming from the stovepipe and a smell of food wafting through the open door. The old man seemed to be preparing his midday meal.

He greeted them cheerfully and looked exactly the same as the last time they met. His hands were still thick with grime as he put more bacon in the skillet and heaped beans on their plates.

'I ain't got no bread,' he said with the regret of any good host, 'but what's here is as tasty as you'd get in any fancy hotel. And I make the kinda coffee that sure keeps a fella together.'

He reached up to the shelf and took down his Sunnyside tin to add to the brew already on the lower plate of the stove. It smelt good and the three men eventually sat down to an enjoyable meal.

'Havin' any luck?' Marshal Willard asked as they ate.

'Nary a thing,' the old man said sadly. 'I'm thinkin' of movin' on up around the Gila. There's still a few spots worth tryin' out that way. But this place is finished. I ain't makin' drinkin' money outa it. So, tell me, what is you two fellas doin' back in Dryburg? I don't reckon you for the sight-seein' types.'

Phil Willard explained the recent happenings and the old man listened quietly. He cheered up considerably when he heard of Brad Webster's death and nodded his understanding as the marshal spoke.

'Well, I can't say as I'm any sorta trackin' fella,' Seth said after a bit of thought, 'but I weren't brought up in no city neither. They'd gone when I got back here, like I said, and the only things they'd left behind were scraps of food and a jar of corn mash as a little present for me. You mentioned their rig, and I figure there certainly was one. It left here movin' due west. In the direction of Fremont, I figure.'

'Not south, towards the border?'

'Hell, no. Clear tracks outa town towards the west. One rig pulled by a mule, and two horses bein' ridden.'

Phil Willard's mouth dropped open a little.

'Two horses!' he exclaimed. 'Are you sure?'

'Sure I'm sure. Workin' mules is shod different from ridin' horses.'

'That don't make sense,' Bill said softly.

There was silence round the table and Phil Willard's coffee grew cold as he tried to puzzle out the situation.

'Any other ideas, Seth?' he eventually asked.

'Can't think of none. You stayin' the night?'

'I reckon so. We'll be headin' back to Cooper's Creek to see if any news has come through on the telegraph or if the local marshal has heard anything.'

'Pitch up at the jailhouse again then,' Seth advised. 'It's the only decent place in town.'

Phil Willard grinned.

'You'd miss Dryburg if you left, Seth,' he said. 'You've gotten yourself a sort of kingdom of your own here. No boss-man, and nobody to make trouble for you.'

The old man nodded as he accompanied them to the door.

'Happen you're right there,' he agreed, 'and I'm feelin' too old to move. But I gotta make a living, and lookin' for gold is all I knows in life. That's the trouble with fellas like me. We always think that some day we're gonna hit the big one.'

They were standing at the door of the little cabin and Phil Willard scanned the long ridges of gaping tunnels and heaps of spoil that disfigured the area and ruined the water supply to destroy the little town.

'Was that where they got their copper?' he asked.

'Hell, no,' Seth said angrily. 'Them tunnels is where fellas was diggin' out gold ten or twelve years back. The copper miners was over beyond that ridge. Steam shovels, they had, and blastin' powder. They dug a few tunnels back there, lookin' for the stuff, I reckon. But once they found it, they tore the hillside apart. All the waste ended up in the creek and it finished this place. Folk just had to move away.'

'So where is you workin' now, Seth?'

'I've been clearin' some of the creek and pannin' it. Ain't much to show for the work though. I'm gettin' a mite tired of it all.'

'Did you never try those old tunnels?

Maybe hit on a new vein?'

'Sure did. And I got a few small bits and pieces in that one just above the old burial plot. Then I just had to stop workin' it. Some coyotes had taken somethin' up there and left it to rot. The stink was worse'n I ever did come across. I dunno what they dragged into that tunnel, but it sure was past eatin' time for it.'

Marshal Willard looked at Bill and took Seth gently by the arm.

'When did this happen, Seth?' he asked quietly.

The old man scratched his head.

'Well, I was workin' there when the fellas rode in and paid me to spend a few days away from town. It was when I comes back that it happened. I went up there to start work and the smell was pretty strong. I tried again a coupla days later, but it were worse. Real dead smell, it were . . . '

Seth suddenly seemed to realize what he was saying. He stared at the two men and there was a silence while all three started to move slowly towards the old burial ground.

'But them folks left,' Seth said in a small voice. He turned to the federal man. 'Is you reckonin' on there bein' some sorta shoot-out and folk is buried there?'

'That might have happened, Seth. Is there a lamp in the tunnel?'

'Hell, no. I'll go back and get one. But I ain't goin' in the place unless that stink has shifted itself. It was one almighty big smell, but I never did think of fellas bein' in there. Just somethin' the coyotes had killed and laid down while I was away. Just wait for me.'

He hurried back to the cabin while Bill and the lawman looked at the long row of tunnel mouths in silence. Seth was soon back again, waving an oil lamp and a couple of candles. The three walked towards the ridge and began climbing the rough ground until they reached the mouth of the tunnel that the old prospector had indicated. There was still a slight smell coming from it, but not bad enough to bother Phil Willard. He took out a vesta and lit the lamp.

The other two stood by the entrance, and as if by mutual consent, they let him enter alone. Old Seth peered into the gloom at the receding figure that was bent nearly double in the cramped space. Bill stayed in the open air. He did not feel like being too near decayed corpses and the slight smell was enough to deter him.

It was several minutes before the marshal returned. His face was streaked with dirt and his hands were grimy as he lifted the glass to put out the lamp. He looked at the two men and nodded his head grimly.

'There are four of them in there,' he said in a low voice. 'Two men and a coupla women. The bodies are too far gone to identify but I reckon it's the driver, the guard, and the two passengers. Brad Webster's wife is dead.'

'And the money?' Bill had to ask the question although it seemed a heartless thing to do.

Phil shook his head. 'Not a bent cent. Even the rings are missin' off their fingers. Everythin' of value has been taken, and I reckon to know who did it.'

He turned to old Seth who was peering anxiously into the mouth of the tunnel as though waiting for a ghost to appear.

'You know Fremont, Seth,' the marshal said in his official voice. 'Ever met a fella from there by the name of George Brent?'

The old man nodded vigorously. 'Sure have. He's one nasty sort of coyote, is George Brent. Buys and sells horses and mules without as much as spittin' in the direction of the brand. And that crooked brother-in-law of his is just as bad. If you come across them two, shoot first and start talkin' to 'em later.'

'Brent is already dead. He met up

with young Bill here. So this brother-in-law. That's Dale Braden we're talkin' of?'

'That's right. Little fat fella what looks like he should be teachin' school or tendin' Bible class.'

'I've met him,' Bill said quietly.

Marshal Willard handed the lantern to Seth.

'You'll be meetin' him again, Bill,' he said. 'I figure as how he's the man who has what we're lookin' for.'

The lawman turned to walk away from the tunnel. He and Bill slithered their way down the slope of rattling shale while old Seth dithered uncertainly at the dark entrance.

'What am I supposed to do about the folk in there?' he shouted. 'I ain't no mortician, and I sure as hell don't figure on sayin' words over nobody. I ain't the prayin' sort.'

'They'll keep,' the marshal said sadly. 'We'll tell the folks in Cooper's Creek and they'll arrange for them to be picked up and buried decent.'

'Well, the quicker, the better,' the old man snorted. 'I ain't used to company in this town. Coyotes is friendlier than most of the folks I seem to meet.'

13

Fremont had not changed since Bill Pearce last rode down the rutted main street. The dirty windows of the saloon still displayed an unwelcoming face and the marshal's office remained closed. He and Phil Willard called in at the saloon for a drink. There were only two other customers there and they were sitting at a table in deep conversation.

The bartender looked sharply at Bill as he passed across the beers. His eyes held a puzzled expression.

'I seen you before,' he said.

'Yeah. I shot George Brent.'

The man cheered up a little. 'Yeah, and you did the town a big favour,' he said. 'And now we got rid of that brother-in-law of his as well. Maybe we gotta thank you for that.'

'I don't reckon so, but he was the fella I wanted to see. Where's he gone?'

The man looked across at the other two patrons but they were not listening.

'Just vanished one night,' he said mysteriously. 'Left his wife runnin' the business. She ain't sayin' nothin' but some folk reckon as how she might have killed him. After all, George Brent was her brother and Dale went round lookin' too pleased with himself at his death. He got all the money so it was a real good shootin' you did as far as Dale Braden was concerned.'

Marshal Willard leaned across the bar. 'I thought George Brent had a wife,' he said. 'Didn't she get his business and the money?'

'Hell, no. She walked out on him years ago and took the kids with her. Folk don't even know where she is. Dale just went and collared everythin' in sight. Now his wife has it all, I reckon. She's runnin' the horse-dealin' business and the rig outfit. If she's killed him, then she's the richest woman in town.'

The bartender gave directions to Ma

Braden's place when asked and then leaned forward confidentially. He addressed Bill.

'Was you figurin' on shootin' Dale?' His voice was eager.

'Figurin' on arrestin' him,' Marshal Willard answered as he showed his badge.

'What's he done?' The man was avid for gossip.

'A few killings and a spot of robbery.'

'I told you him and George was no good, but I figure as how you're too late. I'll lay odds his old lady has beaten you to it.'

He chuckled at the thought and watched the two men leave. Then he crossed to the table to break the latest news to his other customers. They all had a good laugh and one of them winked at the bartender.

'Did you tell them fellas about Ma Braden's guard dog?' he asked.

The saloon man shook his head. 'I ain't one for spoilin' the fun,' he said as they all laughed again. 'They'll find out about him when they get their asses bitten.'

Phil Willard and Bill walked down the street and along the alley as they had been directed. Bill pointed out the corral and shed where he had found the mule and shot George Brent. The large barn that housed the rigs for sale was just a few yards away. A name was painted on a board above the wide gates, but age and neglect had eroded the thing away until only a few letters could be seen.

The double gates of the shed were open and Phil Willard put his head in to look around. There were a couple of heavy carts and a small surrey parked there. Pieces of saddlery hung from hooks on the wooden walls while a dismantled two-wheel rig occupied one dark corner.

'Ain't nobody around,' the marshal said. 'Let's try the house. That fella said it was just back of this place.'

He was just about to lead the way when a thought suddenly struck him.

He stopped in his tracks and looked at Bill.

'Maybe I got me a nasty, suspicious nature,' he said slowly, 'but I don't feel as how a town without law is quite the place for a business run by a woman. Agreed?'

Bill nodded. 'So she's got some help?' he suggested.

'Yeah. It would make sense. Let's play this for safety. Us lawmen don't get no medals for bein' heroes.'

Marshal Willard was alone when he approached the neat house behind the barn. He opened the tiny wicket gate and walked sedately up the cinder path to the white door. The little brass knocker seemed ridiculous in his large hand as he rapped for admittance.

The door opened after only a moment and the lawman almost fell backwards a pace as he confronted the figure that stood before him.

The man was huge. He filled the doorway with his bulk and towered above the marshal. His face was hard and tanned, with several days growth of prickly beard. His reddish lips seemed to shine in the dark mass and his narrow eyes glared at the lawman as he stood with a .44 Colt in one strong hand.

'What would you be wantin' here, fella?' The voice was hoarse and unfriendly.

Phil Willard produced his badge. 'I'm makin' a few enquiries in Fremont,' he said meekly, 'and I'd like a few words with Mrs Braden.'

'We ain't got no marshals in this town,' the man said without moving. 'We manage our own law now, so go ride your horse off a cliff. You ain't disturbin' Ma Braden. She's got enough worries.'

Marshal Willard was beginning to recover his poise.

'And suppose I don't?' he asked.

'Then I'll kill you. That badge don't have no meanin' round here.'

'I'm not a town marshal, fella. I'm a federal marshal. So just tell Ma Braden

I'm here before I put you across my knee and tan your thick hide.'

The man stared unbelievingly for a moment. Nobody spoke to him like that and he raised the gun as his thumb pulled back the hammer. Phil Willard had already seen the figure of Bill Pearce coming up behind the man and his words were intended to keep attention focused on himself. There was no sign of a woman trying to stop Bill, and he had come through the back door as the two planned.

Bill poked the barrel of his own Colt firmly into the back of the large man.

'Drop it,' he said quietly.

There was a moment of hesitation and then the big fellow swung round with a roar that brought a stream of saliva from the red-lipped, gaping mouth. Marshal Willard pulled his own gun and fired one shot into the massive chest. The man stared at him for a moment as though not believing that such a thing could happen. He tried to use the Colt but the lawman dashed it out of his hand. It clattered on to the porch as the owner slumped against the white door and streaked it with his blood.

'You played that all wrong,' Phil Willard told Bill. 'Always shoot 'em first and warn them after. You'll never make a successful lawman if you're dead.'

He stepped over the fallen giant and entered the house.

'Where's Ma Braden?' he asked as he holstered his gun.

'In the kitchen. She was workin' there when I broke in. Scared to hell, she is, and not like to make any trouble. I'll go fetch her and make some coffee for us all. What about him?'

He nodded towards the dying man on the floor. The marshal shrugged.

'That shot will bring a crowd around any minute now. They can cart him off to the mortician or to the doctor. Whichever serves best. I'll just wait here until they arrive. One sight of a federal badge and I figure they'll all want to be on their ways elsewhere. You go look after Ma Braden. She's got some questions to answer.'

It was nearly twenty minutes before the crowd dispersed and Marshal Willard was able to sit down in the warm room opposite Mrs Braden. She was a small, stocky woman with a pale, unlined face and neat grey hair. She had recovered from shock now and held a cup of coffee between her tiny hands. She seemed eager enough to talk to the lawman.

'He just up and left me,' she said. 'With every cent we owned. But I reckon I'm lucky to be rid of the bad-tempered brute. I still got the livery stable and George's horse-dealin' business, so I can at least make a livin' without lookin' to other folk for help.'

She looked towards the closed front door where the body of the big man had lain such a short time ago.

'It's a pity about little Eddy though,' she sighed. 'He was a good worker and I felt safe with him around.'

Phil Willard nodded his sympathy

and murmured a few kind words. Then he got down to business.

'Where is your husband now, Mrs Braden?' he asked.

She shrugged. 'Safe from the law,' she said regretfully. 'Dale was never a fool, Marshal. Him and George was two real crafty fellas. They did a lot of business across in Mexico. Sold animals there with awkward brands. Or bought there and sold over here. My sister, Dorothy, always reckoned they kept a coupla women there as well. A little place south of Nogales, it is. They got corrals and a few cattle down there. Always ready in case the law got too close. That's where he'll be hidin' now. I'll lay odds on it.'

'What do you know about Dryburg?' the marshal asked in a quiet voice.

'I know all about it, and I'm right ashamed. Dale and George was always crooked, but I never reckoned Dale for a killer. Even boasted about it, he did, when he brought all that money home.'

'Tell me,' Phil urged.

'Well, this fella rode into town with four mules. He sold three of them to George and then came across to buy a small rig from Dale. It was surely a strange happening. George and Dale talked about it when the fella left town. And then Dale recognized the brands on the mules. He'd seen them on some that were contracted to draw the Tombstone stage. They decided to tail the fella in the rig, and they saddled up and left town.'

She swallowed some coffee. Her voice was getting a little edgy now and the two men waited patiently for her to recover her poise.

'They were gone a few days, and when they got back here, you never did see two happier fellas. They was rich, Marshal. Real rich.'

She shook her head sadly and put down her empty cup on the low side table.

'Then along comes some young fella and kills George. My Dale couldn't get across the street quick enough. He took over the business, grabbed every dollar he could find, and then lit out. He used our best rig, one horse to pull it, and two more in tow. He sure weren't gonna wait round for any law to arrive or for the young fella to come back again.'

Phil Willard suppressed a grin. 'And you think he's gone to this place south of Nogales?' he asked.

'Sure as shootin' fish in a barrel. The spread is called Las Colinas. Whatever that means. I don't rightly know where it is, but somewhere south of Nogales is somethin' he let drop one night when he was drunk. I reckon as how he's settled down there with some Mexican woman. She's welcome to him.'

She looked hard at the two men. 'You goin' after him?' she asked.

Phil looked at his companion and received a nod. 'I reckon so,' he replied.

The two men rode out of town a short time later. People stared at them as they passed down the main street, but there was no hostility and maybe even a grudging admiration on one or two faces. The federal marshal had decided against spending the night in Fremont. They made camp well away from the place and headed south in the morning.

★   ★   ★

It took four days of hot and dusty travelling to cross the border, stock up on food in Nogales, and then move on towards the small ranch. The Mexicans had been helpful and they were sent on their way with accurate directions towards the Valley of the Mists where it was to be hoped that Dale Braden was taking refuge.

The place was neatly laid out. A small adobe ranch house in clean whiteness stood out in the strong sunlight. There were stables nearby and a large barn. A few cattle grazed on the sparse grass and smoke rose from an iron pipe behind the house. The clean windows reflected the sun and there was a wide porch with cane chairs scattered about it.

Two middle-aged women worked at a well, pummelling clothes and hanging them out to dry on a couple of lines that stretched between buildings. A child played near a horse trough and a Mexican man in white shirt and large sombrero chopped wood in a far corner near what looked like a small workshop.

There was a moment of doubt in the marshal's eyes as he took in the scene from the top of the long, barren slope. Then he saw something that relieved his fears. A large northern surrey was in the lee of one of the stables. Some saddles lay across a fence and they were not the high-pommelled Mexican type. He also spotted something else and pointed out the figure reclining on the porch.

Bill shaded his eyes to look, and smiled as he saw the large belly of Dale Braden rise and fall rhythmically.

'That's our man,' he said.

14

Dale Braden was cautious. An instinct seemed to wake him as the two men watched from the top of the rise. He roused from a fitful doze and peered across the wide space to where the figures were visible in the slight heat haze. He let out a muffled curse and scrambled to his feet. The two women saw what was happening, noted the newcomers, and fled towards the house. The old man and the child followed them. They almost beat Dale Braden at getting through the doorway. The loud noise of it slamming against the world could be clearly heard by Bill Pearce and the marshal as they rode towards the building.

The blast of the shotgun was almost drowned by the noise of their animals over the pebbly ground. It was too great a range and they were in no danger. But it was a warning that Dale Braden was not going to be taken without a fight. Shutters were slamming across the insides of the windows and two guns peeked between them to take more careful aim.

There were more blasts from shotguns as the two intruders jumped from their horses and took shelter behind the well. The washing still fluttered in the light breeze and some shirts lay across the stonework with a bar of yellow soap on top of them. Marshal Willard took aim with his Winchester and put a bullet neatly through the gap between two of the shutters. The shotgun barrel wavered wildly before being levelled again.

Bill was covering the other window. The shotgun there had vanished and the barrel of another weapon appeared. It seemed to be an old rifle and went off with the dull explosion of black powder. The shot chipped away a large piece of stone a couple of feet away from the young man's head.

'How many do you reckon are in there?' Bill asked the marshal as he reloaded.

'I reckon them two women and the old fella are helpin' out,' the marshal growled. 'I sure as hell saw a fancy sleeve just now. He might have some ranch hands close by, so we'd better watch our backs.'

Another shot from the house took a further chip from the stonework of the well and both men had to duck. Bill caught a quick glimpse of the marksman as the gun was withdrawn for reloading.

'The old man's sure in there,' he told the marshal. 'He's the one with the rifle. How long are we gonna be stuck here?'

The lawman shrugged. 'As long as it takes, I reckon. It'll be dark in a coupla hours and then I'll use the old tried and trusted way of gettin' results. We'll burn 'em out.'

'That place is adobe with a tiled roof,' Bill pointed out. 'How in hell do you start a blaze there?'

Phil Willard grinned and indicated a small barrow near one of the sheds.

'A pile of kindlin' in that and a quick push onto the porch is all it takes,' he said. 'The stoop and the roof above it are made of wood and as dry as could be. The front of the place will go up in smoke and they'll panic. I've used tricks like that a few times. Like I said, lad, marshallin' ain't about playin' at brave soldier-boys. It's about low cunnin' and survivin' to retire with a few dollars.'

'So we just keep their heads down for now?'

'Yeah. There's no point in takin' risks.'

Something was happening as he spoke and the two men stared at the building in front of them. A rifle barrel had been poked out of one of the windows and a white flag that seemed to be torn off a piece of bedding was waving at them frantically.

'Well, I'm damned,' the marshal muttered as he stared at the house and watched the door opening slowly. Three guns were thrown out and clattered onto the porch. Then two women and the elderly Mexican emerged fearfully and stood in the open, their hands raised and their faces pale. A little boy followed them, hiding behind the skirts of one of the women.

'Cover me, lad,' the marshal ordered as he went forward and spoke to the man in passable Spanish. Bill watched the windows for any sign of movement while the lawman seemed satisfied and entered the house. He emerged a moment or two later, said something to the little Mexican group, and then crossed to Bill.

'We've been had, fella,' he said savagely. 'Taken for a coupla prize asses. There's a corral out back with one horse ready to make a run. Dale Braden emptied the safe in there, got out through a rear window, and is off south. He paid these folks ten dollars each to do a bit of wild shootin' until he was clear. Ten dollars is a lotta money to poor folks. We'd better get movin' after him.'

The two men went to collect their horses while the three Mexicans retreated to a bunkhouse and congratulated themselves on survival. Dale Braden had told them to hold out until nightfall. He had overlooked human nature and now only had about half an hour start on the law.

'Are you sure we're doin' the right thing?' Bill asked as they rode away from the ranch. 'There's one hell of a lotta places he could be headin' for.'

The marshal's eyes were on the wild country ahead. He was watching every ridge and track as he turned to speak.

'He can't risk us takin' him home to be tried,' he shouted, 'and he can't double back to Nogales because it's too near the border. His safest bet is to head for Magdalena. It's only a small place but they got law there. Mexican law. And the Mexicans who run things really hate our guts. All he has to do is to pay them a few dollars and there's no way they'll be handin' him over. He's got things well figured out, has Dale Braden. So we gotta catch up with him mighty fast.'

His eyes were back on the trail ahead, but he turned his head once more.

'And if you do get a chance of a shot at him,' he yelled above the noise of hoofs and wind, 'aim for the horse. It's one hell of a bigger target. Don't go all sentimental on me.'

They travelled for nearly an hour before a slight haze of dust appeared near a line of low-growing cactus plants that stood below a sand dune. Something had disturbed the wildlife there. Bill did not need the marshal to point out the birds that flew around in an agitated fashion. The wind soon blew the dust away but they turned their horses in that direction and spurred them on.

Then they saw him. Dale Braden's animal was just visible between some yuccas that climbed towards a ridge. They could see the rider clearly as he urged his mount up the slope to be out of sight at the other side. He had left it too late and his pursuers let out little gasps of triumph as they speeded up their own mounts.

It was another twenty minutes or so before they were within shooting range. Marshal Willard pulled up his horse and unholstered the Winchester.

'You keep ridin' after him,' he shouted. 'I'll dismount and take a few shots from here. If I miss, then at least one of us will still be in the hunt. And keep outa my line of fire. I want to aim steady from a kneelin' position. Just like a good soldier-boy.'

Phil Willard dismounted and levered a cartridge into the barrel of the Winchester. He knelt on the sandy ground and took careful aim at the distant figure. The marshal was a good marksman but slightly out of breath. His pull on the trigger was gentle and he swore in surprise when the shot missed.

He re-cocked the weapon and took

aim again. Dale Braden had swung a little to the west and the galloping roan offered a slightly bigger target. He squeezed at the trigger again and let out a whoop of triumph as the animal stumbled. It picked itself up for a moment and then went down on its front legs. The rider scrambled off as it rolled over to one side, kicking its legs wildly.

'Go for him, lad!' the marshal shouted as he holstered the carbine and mounted his horse. Bill was already some twenty yards nearer to the man who was now running across the uneven ground clutching a saddlebag and a shotgun. He stumbled a few times and then caught his foot in some tangled dead roots. He fell amid a mass of small cactus plants.

Bill was on him before he could properly recover. The young man's horse loomed over Dale Braden as the man swung the shotgun round and cocked one of the barrels. He let fly and the animal reared in fright as some of the shot caught it in the head and neck. Bill felt a few of the pellets in his own face and hands as he tried to keep his seat. He drew his .44 and fired at the kneeling man before the shotgun could be used again.

It was a lucky shot and caught Dale Braden high in the chest. He reeled backwards and the gun dropped from his hands. Bill dismounted and ran across to him. The man was still alive and trying to reach out for the fallen gun. Bill kicked it out of the way and took the .45 that Braden had at his waist.

'I'm bad hit,' the man wheezed as he lay with his legs twisted under him. 'You got no rights to go shootin' me, fella. I ain't done nothin' wrong in this territory. No federal marshal's got rights in Mexico.'

'I'm not a marshal,' Bill grinned as he picked up the saddle-bag. 'The fella back there is the lawman. I'm just along for the ride. You should remember me. I killed George Brent. So don't try any more tricks or I'll put another bullet into you.'

Dale Braden stretched out his legs with difficulty and lay silently as he breathed with a rasping sound as slight traces of blood frothed on his lips.

Marshal Willard dismounted and came across to look at the fallen man. He patted Bill on the shoulder and pointed to the saddle-bag.

'Is it all there?' he asked.

Bill opened one of the flaps and took out a large paper parcel. It contained money, and it seemed to amount to several thousand dollars. The two men grinned while Dale Braden eyed them both balefully. There was another parcel of jewellery along with some watches and vesta cases.

'Looks like we hit the jackpot, fella. First prize outa the cracker barrel. Is your stuff there?'

Bill searched carefully but nothing appeared that seemed to remotely resemble the industrial diamonds he needed to find.

'What have you done with them?' he asked Dale Braden as he dumped the saddle-bag angrily on the ground.

The man was slipping into a stunned condition and had to blink rapidly to stay awake. Bill knelt down to catch what he was trying to say.

'Done with what?' he managed to ask in a thin voice.

'The diamonds. Where in hell are they?'

The man seemed to wake up. His eyes focused on the two men who stood over him.

'Diamonds?' he repeated softly. 'I never heard tell of no diamonds. Me and George took every-thin' them folks had with them. We got the lot, and it's all there, fella. You got every last cent and every last trinket of it. But there weren't no diamonds.'

His eyes hardened for a moment.

'Unless George Brent played me for some hick rube. He was no honest dealer, and that's as sure as shooting. He musta pocketed them for himself. I certainly never saw no diamonds except in them brooches and things.'

Marshal Willard had not been paying attention to the exchange. He was checking the contents of the saddle-bag against the official list in his large hand. There was a satisfied smile on his face at a job completed.

'Well, we got most of it,' he said complacently. 'I reckon we can head for Cooper's Creek now and take all the credit.'

'I've been hired to get them diamonds,' Bill said stubbornly. 'And nothin' else concerns me.'

He turned to the injured man.

'They were in a small bag,' he said urgently, 'and addressed to a minin' company, all wrapped up in paper and string. They didn't look important. Just like some collection of rough gravel. Did you see anythin' like that?'

Dale Braden shook his head. He was fading again and not interested in what was going on. Bill stood up and looked at the saddlebag and the happy face of the marshal.

'I ain't finished,' he said grimly. 'If those stones don't turn up, nobody's ever gonna give me a job again. I guess I'm on my own now.'

It was really a question and the lawman nodded sadly.

'You are, son,' he said. 'I gotta get this lot back to where it belongs I'm sure sorry I can't help more. What have you got in mind?'

Bill considered. He looked at the injured man and glanced round at the mountainous and desolate country in which they stood.

'Well, I guess I go back to Dryburg and search that stage again. Maybe nobody noticed the damned things. After all, they weren't supposed to be noticed.'

Phil Willard nodded agreement.

'I reckon that's your best move,' he agreed. 'We'd better bed down here for the night. This fella ain't gonna last much longer and we got enough food and water to manage well enough. I'll also take them bits of shot outa your hide before you start lookin' like a prickly pear. Let's unsaddle the animals and rest our bones. We've surely earned our supper this day.'

15

Dale Braden died during the night. They buried him as best they could in the soft, sandy ground. Then the marshal piled some rocks and dead brushwood over the site to try and keep prowling animals away. He knew it was really useless, but the effort had to be made.

The two men rode north again and stopped at a small Mexican settlement for more food. The lawman was jubilant and had been careful to get a home address from Bill so that his share of any rewards would not go astray. They parted company just north of Nogales, Marshal Willard heading towards Cooper's Creek and Bill steering for Dryburg.

There was still a journey of several days to the deserted town and the young rider had to endure the intense heat and sudden biting cold of the semi-desert conditions. The wind cut his face, sharp with fine sand and grit that blew from the western slopes. It was with a sigh of relief that he finally topped a rise and saw the dilapidated ruin of Dryburg again. He almost grinned at the idea that he would ever be glad to see such a place.

There was no sign of Seth, and Bill was too impatient to go looking for the old man. He headed straight for the smithy where the coach was stored and entered through the rotting doors. It was still there, covered in dust and looking as ancient as the rest of the town.

He climbed onto the driver's seat and searched with a careful precision. The parcel of diamonds would only be a small thing that could be tucked away under a seat or down a gap where the water bottles were kept. It could easily have been over-looked in the first search. He found nothing and cursed as he jumped down to look inside the vehicle. The door opened easily and he climbed up into the interior with its leather seats and luggage racks. The seats came out and the young searcher threw them from the coach in his growing frustration.

A shadow suddenly fell across him and he reached down automatically for the gun at his side. Old Seth stood in the doorway. He held a shotgun and peered into the gloom of the building with short-sighted eyes.

'Oh, it's you, young fella,' he cried cheerfully as he lowered the gun. 'Thought I'd gotten myself some trouble-makin' varmints in town. What you lookin' for?'

Bill scrambled out of the stage and wiped his hands. He told Seth of the events that had occupied the last few days. The old miner listened with widening eyes as the tale was unwrapped. He led the way from the smithy to his little cabin and put the coffee pot on the stove.

'You law fellas sure have one

interestin' life,' he said with a certain admiration. 'Beats lookin' for gold. So what was you after on the stage? You searched it well enough when you was here last.'

Bill hesitated. He was not quite sure how much he could trust the old-timer.

'There was a small parcel that we ain't found,' he said carefully. 'Ain't worth much but the owners will want it back. You know how these things are. It could have been overlooked real easy.'

'Well, them fellas didn't leave nothin' worth while that I could see,' Old Seth said as he ladled ground coffee from the large Sunnyside tin. 'They sure as hell emptied that stage. All I got was this coffee and a few tin plates and mugs. There was some food but I threw it away.'

He patted the large tin affectionately as he put it back on the shelf.

'That was the real prize,' he said proudly. 'Full to the brim with real coffee and smellin' right good. I'll be sorry when it's all gone and I have to go back to grindin' beans again.'

He sat down and a sudden look of puzzlement came over his face as he glanced up at the tin.

'Funny thing though,' he said slowly. 'Some fella had put a bag of gravel in it.'

Bill swallowed noisily. 'Seth,' he said in a small and careful voice, 'tell me about the gravel.'

Bill felt he knew now what had happened. Some company agent had tipped the driver a few dollars to hide the diamonds and had not thought to report back to his bosses.

The old man got up to stir the heating coffee. He stood with the spoon in his gnarled hand and an odd look on his face.

'Well, when I opened the tin and saw all this real store coffee, I couldn't believe my luck,' he chuckled. 'I'd been usin' it for a week or so before the spoon hits somethin' that ain't quite right. It was a paper parcel with the name of that goddam minin' company that ruined this town. I opens it up, I does, and there's a leather pouch full of pebbles. Oddest thing I ever did see. The leather pouch was sure a handsome piece of work though. I keeps my baccy in it now. When I've got any.'

'And the pebbles?' Bill asked edgily.

'Well, young fella, that was my revenge,' the old man chuckled. 'I reckon they was samples, tellin' the copper company what sorta ground they would be diggin' up to hurt some other poor town. So I thought about all the folks what lost their homes in Dryburg. And I got rid of them stones.'

Old Seth went over to the window and looked out at his little kingdom.

'I might never strike real money, son,' he said in a gentle voice, 'but I reckon as how that was the richest moment of my life.'

'What did you do with them, Seth?' Bill's voice was a hoarse whisper verging on panic.

The old man winked broadly enough to make his eyes water.

'Dropped 'em down the privy,' he chortled.

There was a long pause as Bill crossed to the rear window and looked at the little wooden building a few yards away.

'And have you cleaned out the privy, Seth?' he asked softly.

'Hell, no. I ain't doin' jobs like that. There's plenty more places in town. Why the hell you askin' such a question, anyways, fella?'

'Oh, I just wondered what sorta diggin' job we got ahead of us.'

THE END

We do hope that you have enjoyed reading this large print book.

Did you know that all of our titles are available for purchase?

We publish a wide range of high quality large print books including:
**Romances, Mysteries, Classics
General Fiction
Non Fiction and Westerns**

Special interest titles available in large print are:
**The Little Oxford Dictionary
Music Book, Song Book
Hymn Book, Service Book**

Also available from us courtesy of Oxford University Press:
**Young Readers' Dictionary
(large print edition)
Young Readers' Thesaurus
(large print edition)**

For further information or a free brochure, please contact us at:
**Ulverscroft Large Print Books Ltd.,
The Green, Bradgate Road, Anstey,
Leicester, LE7 7FU, England.
Tel:** (00 44) 0116 236 4325
Fax: (00 44) 0116 234 0205